R O B E R T

COMPLETELY RESTORED

For Sale – Beautiful 3-story
Victorian house in need of
TLC. Perfect for restoration.
Seller motivated.

Call 641-555-0146

If book discussion group questions are desired, go to the author's webpage:
www.myrobertkerr.com

ISBN: 1-4392-5595-4
ISBN-13: 9781439255957

Visit https://www.createspace.com/1000251356 to order additional copies.

DISCLAIMER

This is a work of fiction. Names, characters, places, and incidents either are products of the author's imagination or are used fictitiously. Any resemblance to actual persons, living or dead, business establishments, events, or locales is entirely coincidental.

DEDICATION

This story is dedicated, to my wife Joan whose love of houses of all types but one house in particular gave me the idea.

In addition I am indebted to a long list of people who aided me along the way, including but not limited to: Shelly Bosovich, whose encouragement spurred me on; Jamie Sawin, who served as my sometimes muse; Richard and Marlys Huff who provided ample references on Marshalltown history; and Dr. Tim Colby who provided technical advice.

"'Mid pleasures and palaces though we may roam, be it ever so humble, there's no place like home."

— John Howard Payne (1791 - 1852)

CHAPTER I

June 5, 2009

ISRAEL HOPES OBAMA

SPEECH WILL LEAD TO PEACE

It was June 5, 2009. Nate and Abby stood silently at my side, tears flowing freely down their faces, as I comforted Sammy Jo. The kids had been through so much; we all had!

Riverside Cemetery is a beautiful place in June, with its stately old trees, gently rolling knolls, and centuries old headstones, but not on that day. Riverside was just another reminder of what had happened in the past several months, a reminder none of us needed: poor little Sammy Jo!

As I held her, she buried her face in my shoulder and sobbed. I had no words with which to console her, relying instead on the sounds and pats that had always soothed her hurts in the past. Linda would probably have had answers for Sammy Jo, and Abby and Nate, but I had nothing to offer but my own anguish.

I realized the crowd was thinning. Only the sounds of dress shoes on gravel, shutting car doors, and starting motors competed with the silence of the graveyard. "Come on kids," I said as I steered them toward the car, "Let's go be with your mother." I kept thinking none of this would have happened if not for that Goddamn house!

I have to confess how much I envy fiction writers; they can shape the story and create or distort facts as they see fit to make it easier to tell, easier to believe. Our story is unbelievable, and hell, I don't actually *believe* it and I *lived* through it. If not for the fact that all five of us report exactly the same memories of the experience, I'd think it was a dream. Actually, I'd prefer that, but the facts say otherwise. I must tell the story sequentially, in the same order that time revealed it to us. Besides, I promised Linda that if I ever decided to tell anyone what happened to us, I would be as truthful as possible. And so I will.

Our time in Marshalltown had been good to us. Linda and I had three reasonably normal kids and one very odd dog. We would have had four kids, but, well, things happen. After that, Linda changed. She still had those moments of impishness when she would turn the slightest thing into a giggle and the giggle into convulsive laughter for both of us. She still had those moments, but they were a lot farther apart.

I thought that was how we became interested in the house in the first place. I thought Linda was looking for something to fill the void, when she saw the ad for the "beautiful 3-story Victorian house in need of some TLC." We had admired the house from a distance for years, but never dreamed it could be ours. One peek inside and that look returned to Linda's face for the first time since, well, since the baby.

We had had other fixer-uppers before, but this one was different from the very beginning. It needed more work than any of the others to be sure, but there was something else. It was as if the house pulled at our whole family. It was as if fate meant for us to live in *that* house. For one thing, all of our antiques fit perfectly into every room. We had just the right furniture and accent pieces for each room right down to the fully outfitted dress mannequin Linda kept in our bedroom. (I never got used to the idea of sex with *her* looking on.) After researching the pattern at the local library, Linda found the perfect china in an antiques shop. The house even had the right number of bedrooms for our family of five. Everything was perfect. Our 1908 Victorian was *the* house for showing off our antiques and collections, for reviving our passion for old things, for deepening our obsession with what we thought was a better time. The house was the perfect drug for our addiction. It was a match! It wasn't a match made in heaven, however.

From the day we took possession of the house, Linda took charge. She cleaned, scrubbed, waxed and straightened. She made lists—lists of things to buy, things to fix, and things for me to do. By the end of that first summer, we had settled in, but we certainly weren't finished. By the first Christmas, I knew that Linda wasn't going to slack off until she had completely restored the house to its original 1908 glory from the cellar floor all the way up to the weather vane on top of the roof. At first, I thought finances would force some restraint; as educators, we didn't make much money. Time had an answer for that too when it ran out for Linda's great-Aunt Mary late in 2007. Linda inherited enough dough to have put all of the kids through Iowa State: twice! All that money went right into the house.

As our money trickled into the house, our time poured into it as if it were some sort of time-sucking abyss. The summer we roofed and painted the house, we barely saw the kids or anyone else for that matter. Of course, Sammy stayed confined to our yard, but Abby and Nate left shortly after they were dressed and never returned until long after we were in bed. The house took over our lives and we just went along for the ride. By the time we were reaching the end of the restoration in the spring of 2009, we could not have predicted where that ride would take us.

I'll never forget how it started; it was the first day of summer vacation in 2009. Only those who earn their living entertaining other people's kids with history lessons, Shakespeare, and story problems can understand the splendid sense of relief that comes with the first day of summer vacation. I've always judged the quality of the summer to come by the way the sun comes up on that first day after we've gained our release from the bonds of educational servitude. That Friday the sunrise was a beauty! I remember lying in bed next to Linda, absolutely loving that we had the next 10 weeks to enjoy any way we chose.

On that first morning of summer, I looked forward to completing the one last detail of the restoration of

314 W. Main Street and spending the rest of my summer enjoying the house and my family. After all, I had spent every free hour of the past three years addressing Linda's every whim when it came to the restoration.

Some men might have objected to such an arrangement with their wives, but I respected our differences in talents and had learned years before that Linda had very good instincts about such things. When I stepped back and let her make those decisions and found ways to make her ideas work, all three of us—Linda, me, and the house—were better off. Besides, Linda always felt free to show her appreciation.

I wondered that first morning in June how she knew I had been staring as she drew the sheet up over her nakedness and turned over to wish me good morning. However, thoughts of the day's work interrupted her kiss. "You remember you have to go get the door from Hank today," Linda reminded me.

"I know, I know," I yawned in response. "I told him I would come out about 10 this morning. I took the sugar pine frame materials and hardware with me last time and conned him into framing the door." This seemed to satisfy her for the moment.

She kissed me again. I was fast closing in on some more of Linda's "attentions" when the bedroom door burst open and in popped Sammy. "Samantha Jo Murphy! You know you're supposed to knock when you come into Mommy and Daddy's room," Linda scolded.

"Sorry," Sammy said as she rapped twice on the wide-open door. "Today's when Daddy's gonna put the door on the house! Then it'll be *all* done, right?"

Like most five-year-olds, Sammy saw no point in concealing excitement or any other feeling for that matter, but she was no more excited about seeing the house completed than we were. For us, the door had represented the final touch in the restoration of the house ever since the first day three years ago when Linda found it covered in dust in the basement behind the monster furnace.

I had wanted to leave the more energy-efficient modern door the Daltons had installed. It was one of those hybrid jobs with the oak veneer on the inside and the vinyl-coated steel outside surface, but Linda had other ideas. Everything else about the house, from the split cedar shingles to the white-washed cellar walls, was authentic, and the original front door was not going to be the exception. End of discussion!

So the door came up from the basement in April and went out to Hank's shop for restoration, and by day's end, it would be mounted in its rightful place on the front entrance, the crown jewel of the restoration. Finally, we would have completely restored the house and we could get down to the business of enjoying our hard work, living in the masterpiece, enjoying each other and our life together. At least that was our plan.

I have always loved being a dad and cannot imagine life without my family, but there have been times when the breakfast hour wasn't my favorite time of day. I have even blown out of the house early just to avoid the rash of complaints, arguments, and generally shitty attitudes that seem to go along with breakfast with two teenagers. It wasn't that I wanted to shirk my fatherly duties; I have always taken my responsibility to parent very seriously, *too* seriously, according to Nate and Abby (and their friends' parents). "You're *too* strict!" "None of our friends have to be in by 11!" "Josh's dad lets him drive the SUV all the time!" I got sick of hearing it and tired of defending my parenting philosophy, particularly to other parents. I mean, raising teenagers would be a lot easier if you could count on the other kids' parents to do it too. I know I'd stand a better chance of seeing crooked politicians lined up at the confessional, but a person can hope, can't he?

Linda was much more realistic about the whole parenting business. While I ragged on Nate and Abby about grades and threatened them with loss of their privileges (if not their limbs), Linda hung a needlepoint sampler which read, "Raising Children Is Like Being Pecked to Death by Chickens!" across from the foot of our bed.

All of this ran through my mind that morning when I saw Abby's car in the middle of the driveway as I went to back my truck out of the garage. I reminded myself about the part poultry could play in my eventual demise when I noticed the crumpled fender. Then, when I realized that I couldn't go anywhere until I charged Abby's dead battery, I shared *all* of the words I had promised Linda I would no longer use with the neighbors at the top of my lungs! Twice! The sticker on Abby's bumper twisted the blade nicely: have a *nice* day, my ass!

CHAPTER 2

As I rounded the corner into Hank's place, I could see the door leaning up against his barn/workshop. Hank wasn't much of a conversationalist and he sort of had a face for radio, but he did know his way around the woodshop. He also had a real knack for restoring the finish on furniture and millwork so that it was pleasing to the eye without destroying its character ("patina" as he called it). People in town called it "Hank's Magic." The door fairly beckoned to me as I pulled to a stop.

Hank had done his usual superb job. All of the layers of paint were gone, the nicks and dings had become beauty marks, the hardware looked better than we had ever imagined it could, and, it was in the frame, ready to install!

"Hank, you've outdone yourself!" I said. "It's absolutely gorgeous!" Hank grinned his famous toothless grin and replied humbly, "Of course. Nothing less for the Murphys!"

As I paid him, he grabbed one side of the door frame and asked "So is this about it for the restoration or will you be bringing me more work?"

"Hank," I replied, "this is it! About two more hours to hang it and we're done!"

"Well, it's been a long haul, but you and Linda have a beautiful house now. And..." Hank started.

"I know, 'They don't make 'em like that anymore,'" I interrupted. "Come on, let's get this beauty in the truck."

With Hank's assistance, I loaded the door and was back in town by 10:30. The house appeared deserted, left in the care of Sarge, who gave me a few obligatory barks before she returned to licking her feet.

It was anybody's guess where Nate or Abby were, but the empty bike rack told me Linda and Sammy were on a ride. As I backed the truck up to the porch, I saw Linda and Sammy coming down the street on their bikes. "Great timing," I said. "I thought I'd have to unload this monster by myself."

"It is Friday, so we had to visit Sammy's angel, you know," Linda explained. Shortly after Linda's great-aunt died, Sammy adopted the grave of baby *Samuel W. Green* who had died at birth. She found it in the Angel's Garden that spring when Linda went to place flowers on her aunt's grave. She had been making weekly visits to it since, leaving bouquets of dandelions or flowers from Linda's nearly deforested garden.

As soon as I pulled off the tarp, I could tell Linda absolutely loved the door. I had prepared myself for her usual conditional praise of Hank's work ("It's really nice, but…"). However, this time Hank had hit the nail squarely on the head. She stood and stared at the door silently as tears formed in her eyes. I wasn't sure if the tears were for Hank's fine work or maybe a bit of sadness since the door was the absolutely last touch and Linda knew it meant no more restoration remained for us to do. On the other hand, maybe the visit to the grave of Sammy's angel stirred still tender memories.

As she helped me walk the door out of the truck and lift it onto the front porch, she finally regained her composure enough to remark, "God, all that paint Hank removed sure didn't weigh much!" We rested the door against the front wall of the house. Sammy put her bike away in the garage and returned with my tool belt and hammer. One look from Linda and I knew my plan of waiting until after lunch to tear out the metal door and rehang the wooden one was toast. We all three pitched in and had the Daltons' door out of the wall in a few minutes. Another hour and I had our restored door back in its rightful place in the main entrance to our house.

After lunch, Linda and I attached the brick molding and the interior trim. By 2:30 we had a fully functional door complete with the original mechanical doorbell operated by a twist handle on the outside center of the door. I was ready to jump on Sammy about how she would wear it out playing with it, but Linda reminded me that since it had lasted 100 years, it probably could take anything Sammy could dish out.

In our haste to get the door restored and back in place, we had overlooked one small, but important, detail. Like all locks from that time, a simple skeleton key worked the mechanism, not the modern type. We always thought the key would turn up somewhere during all the restoration, but it had not and we hadn't bothered to buy a replacement. Until we did, we couldn't operate the lock. Linda seemed almost pleased at the thought— one last thing for her to research and restore!

I picked up tools while Linda and Sammy swept up the sawdust and wood debris. At 4, Nate passed through the restored door on his return from the pool. He charged up the stairs to his room, changed into his clothes, and headed back out the same door to baseball practice without so much as a grunt. He probably wouldn't have noticed at all if Abby's hadn't shrieked, "Where the hell did that come from?" as he passed her on his way out. Nate turned, gave a perfunctory look at the open door, and uttered an approving "Cool!" which was probably aimed more at the fact that I had done something to make Abby swear than at Hank's craftsmanship. Not only had Hank put $400 of his time and my money into it, but it also symbolized the end of our work. The door had not received its due recognition. There was time for that to change.

After dinner, Linda and I discussed several options for what to do about the keyless door. We, actually she, rejected applying any sort of temporary hardware to the door or frame. Nor did she want to use just any key to lock the door for the night. We finally decided to prop it open with a chair so we could enjoy the night breeze and firmly lock the screen door until Linda could find just the right key for the lock in a restorer's catalog. And besides, we all had keys to the back door, so if we had to lock it we could always use that "Club" thingy Dad had given me for Christmas several years earlier.

After Abby's softball game, Linda, Sammy, Abby, and I had pizza while Nate ate at the arcade with his friends from practice. Abby had had three nice hits, but had missed what could have been a game-saving pop fly, so she was in foul mood all through the meal. Sammy did her best to cheer Abby up, which Abby barely tolerated.

Because it was the first night of summer vacation, we pretty much suspended bedtimes all together. Nate came in around 10 complaining of boredom and went straight to his room to play his guitar. He was actually getting very good and seemed to be able to play anything by ear, but our willingness to have him playing in the house depended entirely on his selections. That night he concentrated on what he called a Van Morrison tune, but Linda and I knew it as Tommy Edwards' "It's All in the Game". Abby spent at least an hour on the phone and left in a whirl for Sue's house, where we assumed Sue had some gossip even too good for the phone. We tried to remind her that the front door would be locked when she came home and that she would have to use her key to the back door, but she left in such a hurry, we had no way of knowing if she heard us.

Sammy had fallen asleep on the living room floor watching a video. Linda carried her up the stairs and got her into her PJs. From the porch below Sammy's room, I could hear Linda singing "You Are My Sunshine" to Sammy, the final phase of the ritual that was bedtime for Sammy every night.

Once Sammy was down for the count, Linda and I had a leisurely swing on the front porch. Linda made plans for how we would spend the summer, and I made mental notes about how best to avoid the parts that sounded like work for me. By 11, we decided that having two of the three in the house and accounted for was good enough and that we could steal away to bed and let Abby take care of herself as she had been doing for sometime anyway. Linda seemed to be particularly at peace with the house finally finished. As we readied ourselves for bed, I prayed that she would be content with the house just as it was for a long while so we could finally catch up on some bills. We might even afford one more family vacation trip while all three kids were still at home. Suddenly, Sarge barked that quick, snappy bark that she always used when she realized that the lights are out and she was too. Linda insisted that I go let her in (and at the worst possible moment). I assured her that Abby would let her in when she came home or that Nate would when he crashed for the night. This wasn't the answer she wanted, but the windows were open, there was a nice breeze blowing the scent of lilacs through our bedroom, and we both had better things to think about for the near term.

A few minutes later, Linda kissed me goodnight and rolled over to go to sleep. As usual, I dropped like a rock the minute my head hit the pillow. The next thing I knew, the sound of a door slamming woke me from a very nice dream. I felt Linda stir and I moaned sarcastically, "Nice to see Abby's mood has improved!" Linda answered thoughtfully, "Abby came home 20 minutes ago while you were snoring. And she was singing." Even though I heard her reply, sleep was calling much too loudly for me to make anything of it.

ᕯ

I nearly always wake before anyone else in the house. And I always look forward to that first cup of coffee from the coffeemaker, so I fill it with water and coffee and set the timer just before I go to bed—it's one way I try to stay on Linda's good side. On weekends and vacation mornings, we always start the day with coffee and the paper; it was a pact we made the first week we were married. That morning seemed particularly nice, cool morning air, the birds chirping through the open windows, bright sun. The kind of morning that made me think I could handle anything. And thank God for that!

I put on my summer morning outfit, my favorite t-shirt and some old athletic shorts, and went downstairs. I headed for the front door out of habit to retrieve the newspaper from the porch. Then I realized why I had heard a door slam. The night breezes had blown our beautiful, newly restored door shut in spite of the chair I had placed in front of it to hold it open. The chair which now sat across the entryway from where I had left it and held Abby's purse, shoes, sweatshirt, and the stack of crap she had brought home from her locker the day before. OK, so Abby moved the chair and the door blew shut. No big deal, no harm done. I tried to open the door to get the paper, but no luck. Not only had it blown shut, but also the well-oiled lock mechanism (thanks a bunch, Hank) had clicked into the locked position. I looked out the entryway window for a glimpse of the paper but couldn't see it. I also couldn't see Abby's car, so I instantly wondered how much it was going to cost me to go get the junker and tow it home from wherever it conked out. As I headed for the back door, I became aware that I was walking very quickly and on my heels, a sure sign, according to Linda, that I should calm down and count to 10. I did not. However, as I reached the back door, I realized that I did not hear Sarge whining to be let in and that Abby must have remembered to bring her in after all, so I began to cut her some slack mentally. I threw open the door and jogged around the side of the house to the front porch, stretched for the paper, and whirled around to go back inside when it started to soak in.

In the back of my mind, I had been hearing the ever-increasing sound of horse's hooves on pavement. In my quest for the paper, I had blocked them out, but I couldn't ignore them any longer. I turned to look up the street and realized for the first time that a horse-drawn milk wagon was making its way toward me. The driver nodded obligingly and said, "Morning. How many today?"

"How many what?" I asked, not sure what the joke was supposed to be yet.

"How many bottles of milk?" he answered.

"None! We switched to soy!" I answered with satisfaction at having the last word in this prank. As I was rapidly cataloging the list of people who would go to such extremes for a laugh, I opened the paper and laughed aloud at the date on the front page. I grinned, thinking someone had outdone himself. As I reached the corner of the house, I noticed for the first time that our fully restored and sided carriage house-style garage no longer sported the vinyl siding Linda and I had installed two years ago and I exclaimed for the neighbors and Linda, "What the fuck?!!". I ran to look at the damage but stopped just short of the door when I realized that our fenced in yard was also gone.

"Joe," Linda yelled, "get up here!" I raced through the kitchen door, tossed the paper on the table, and ran up the steps. Linda met me at the top of the stairs. "Look!" she half whispered as she pointed out the window at the street below. For as far as we could see down Main Street, all the way to the town square, there were only horse-drawn vehicles, dozens of them, coming and going out of driveways and back alleys onto a Main Street made of bricks. A Main Street with streetcar tracks running right down the center of it as far as the eye could see in either direction. "What the hell is going on, Joe?" she demanded.

"How should I know?" I replied helpfully. "All I know is I went downstairs to get coffee and the paper and found the new door blown shut and locked because Abby moved the chair. As I went around to the porch, I found all the siding missing from our garage. Then I ran into some Amish geezer trying to sell me milk while I'm trying to get the paper. So I got nothing! I'd think Hank and Larry were up to some sort of huge prank, but even they couldn't pull this off."

"Well, something really weird is going on. The city isn't having a parade today or something is it?" Linda asked.

"And speaking of the paper, it's some reproduction of a 1909 *Times-Republican*. Clever, huh?" I exclaimed as I let things soak in.

"Why isn't there any electricity?" Abby yelled from the bathroom. "I have to do my hair before Jeff comes to take me to the lake."

Linda and I looked at each other and simultaneously took to the stairs. She tugged on the front door and blurted out profanity even I wouldn't use. We both headed for the back door and outside to survey the situation, Linda still in my old football jersey and little else. Everywhere we looked, we saw signs that we were in fact *in* 1909: The trees all looked much younger; where the 1920's vintage elementary school building should have been visible between Sherrings' house and Whites' there was only a weed-filled vacant lot.

One by one Linda and I noticed stores that we could no longer make out along Main Street even though they had been there clear as day 24 hours earlier. As we rounded the corner to the east side of the house we realized the 6-foot privacy fence that used to separate our yard from the Sheerings' was gone and, along with it, Linda's privacy. A spinster-looking woman in a long brown dress with her hair tied up in a bun was staring at Linda's naked lower half, barely covered by my long-ago shrunken jersey. Linda covered herself reflexively and tried to shrink to reduce the exposure. The woman had been hanging laundry but had stopped midway through the hanging of a bed sheet to stare. I suggested Linda go in and check on the kids, and for once, she did not give me any static about it not being exclusively a woman's job. This seemed to break the woman's spell, but her icy stare turned to hot tongue.

"What are you folks doing in the McGrews' house?" she demanded, lowering the bed sheet so that she could place a hand on either hip.

Before I could even comprehend the insanity of what she had asked me, an older male voice intervened. "Now don't bother these nice people, Mrs. Clark. I'm sure they're tired from their long trip."

At this point I was seriously thinking about spouting off something like "What the hell is this, some demented sequel to the Wizard of Oz?" but instead, for some reason, I turned around and found myself looking into the eyes of the speaker. His weathered, time-worn face sported a pencil-thin moustache. His slightly stooped posture placed his shoulder squarely over his large mid-section. I guessed him to be in his early 70s. Normally I'd have proceeded into one of my famous tirades, but for once, something (perhaps the icy stare of Mrs. Clark) told me to just listen and go along with the charade.

He continued, "I know I told you last month that the McGrews are letting their relatives, cousins I think Mr. McGrew wrote, use their house while they are traveling in Europe this year. It must have slipped your mind with all you have to do around here." It bought me some think time, but that's about all judging from the daggers she was shooting him with her eyes.

"Oh my, where are my manners? Allow me to introduce myself. I'm Dr. Silas W. Fischer. And this is my housekeeper, Mrs. Clark."

I briefly considered demanding an explanation, but instead I bit my lip and extended my hand to each of them.

"I believe you're from Indiana, aren't you?" Dr. Fischer went on.

"Ah, yes. That's right, Gary, Indiana," I answered, borrowing from another one of my favorite classic movies. I stopped just short of adding "Conservatory class of '05."

"And do I have it right that you are a cousin of Mr. McGrew's?" he pursued. This guy was incredible.

"Uh, actually he's my wife's cousin. Through marriage," I ad-libbed. I didn't have a clue where this was going, but I kind of liked it, because it was a far better cover story than I was coming up with and frankly, Linda had been no help at all. I stammered out an

"It's nice to meet you. But I need to help my wife, uh, Linda, with the kids." Then I ran around the house to the back door, locking it behind me. Linda, now fully dressed, stood glued to the window eavesdropping on the good Dr. Fischer and Mrs. Clark. While we couldn't actually make out what they were saying, they were clearly having an argument. She kept pointing toward our house, shaking her finger at it as if to say "naughty, naughty, naughty!" He kept patting her on the shoulder and trying to shoo her toward their house. "Where did these people come from and what have they done with the Sherrings? And who were the McGrews?" I asked rhetorically.

"I don't know who *they* are, but the McGrews are the people who built this house! In 1908!" Linda answered.

Just then, Abby held up the paper with the headline "SINS THAT KEEP MEN FROM CHRIST" and asked, "Who the hell is Billy Sunday?"

CHAPTER 3

June 6, 1909

SINS THAT KEEP MEN FROM CHRIST

**Sunday Preaches on Why Men
Do Not Become Christians**

Neither Nate nor Abby bought the idea that our whole house and everything in it had been catapulted somehow back into the early part of the 20th century. They reacted about as I figured they would; Nate pondered quietly and Abby rejected it out of hand. I don't think Linda *really* had accepted it yet either, but in a sick sort of way, she almost seemed to be hoping that it was true. She had that same glint in her eye that she had when we first looked at the house, the one that meant her spirit of adventure had overruled common sense. While I tried to reason with Abby and at least get her to acknowledge that there were certain things she could not do until we found out what was going on (like leave the house in a bikini), Linda slipped quietly up to the bedroom. Nate finally came up with the most damning evidence of all. He pointed out that we seemed to be the only people in Marshalltown who felt anything was at all out of the ordinary. As Abby looked out the window at the citizenry going about their business I could see that she knew Nate was absolutely correct. After a long silence, Abby asked, "Well where's my car then?"

Nate tried to reason with her that a 1980 Pontiac Grand Prix didn't exist in 1909 (and that *hers* had barely existed in 2009). Nevertheless, she couldn't get past the question of whether her insurance covered this and if it didn't, was that my fault for buying "cheap-ass" coverage. I felt the steam rising and was about to lose it, when Linda appeared in the kitchen dressed in the outfit from the mannequin that graced our bedroom. "Well, how do I look?" she asked cautiously.

"Mom, you're wearing some old dead lady's clothes! That's gross!" Nate offered. Abby just stared.

"You're not getting me into anything like that, I'll tell you right now!" Abby offered defensively.

"Where are you going in that?" I demanded, but I already knew the answer. The handbag on her arm told me she intended to go downtown for some serious shopping. It made sense because none of the rest of us could even leave the house unless we got into duds more suitable to the time. "What about money?" I realized suddenly. Linda's face dropped momentarily, but then she put her handbag down and headed up the stairs. Her high-topped shoes slapped the oak stair treads with each step. We could hear her overhead as she scurried down the hall. She stopped outside our bedroom where my framed collection of pre-crash stock certificates hung in the hall. I jumped from my chair to protest, but with each step, I realized more and more that this was a great idea. By the time I reached the bottom of the stairs, all I could offer was, "Well, start with the biggest ones first!" Whenever Linda beat me to a great idea, I had to tweak it a bit—it's what guys do.

"What are you going to buy?" Abby demanded. "Don't be dragging home some dorky dress like that for me. I won't wear it!"

Linda tore off the backing on the frame and slid out the first of the five stock certificates, the one for the Eclipse Mining and Milling Co. As she did, she assured Abby and the rest of us that she would only buy each of us one outfit and that we could then feel free to go shopping for ourselves later. This satisfied Abby somewhat. Nate and I each offered to trust Linda to buy the whole nine yards for us.

Then Nate dropped the next bombshell; we could pass as 1909-ers with the clothes, but what about the inside of the house? Wouldn't anybody who saw our possessions be suspicious? For a second, I wanted to pull all the curtains and blinds shut, but I knew that we couldn't live cooped up like that very long. Nate was right. We needed to strip any telltale hints of the 20th century from every room or at least the downstairs and carry it to the attic. We needed to do it before that nosy Mrs. Clark saw anything to make her more suspicious.

As I looked around the rooms, I could see we had our work cut out; even though Linda had meticulously restored each room according to her research, we still had hundreds of items from modern-day life in every room. "Let's start with the TV, Nate, and the DVD player and all the DVDs. Help me carry them up to the attic. Abby and Sammy, you go through the bookcase and pull everything that looks too new." I don't know why I jumped into it so willingly; I guess I thought any action was better than just waiting around. I complemented myself on giving in to Linda's insistence on 1909-era reproduction appliances; at least the kitchen wouldn't give us away. "Linda, you go ahead and sell that certificate and buy some clothes for us. And you'd better get some candles too in case I can't get the electricity back on. And a key for that damned door."

We watched out the front window as Linda rounded the front of the house and stepped off the curb toward the on-coming streetcar. I wondered what the bounce in her step was due to, and I was afraid it wasn't the shoes. She did seem to blend in very nicely except for the glimmer of the silver wristwatch on her left arm. I almost called her back, but then I saw her slide it off her wrist and drop it into her bag just as the streetcar came to a stop. She was fitting right in and I wasn't sure I liked that.

An hour and a half later, Linda stepped off the streetcar with several neatly wrapped parcels, the smallest of which seemed certain to hold candles, judging from the wax stains coming through the brown paper in hot sun. I hoped it also held a skeleton key. Linda went around to the back door to enter the house. We all greeted her cautiously, curious to know what she found out downtown and anxious to see what she had bought us. For a few seconds the only thing we heard was the tearing of wrapping paper, sort of like Christmas without the giggles and with a whole lot more "Oh, ick!" and "You've got to be kidding."

As soon as the crumpling and tearing subsided, the comments built to a crescendo of complaints: Complaints that Linda quelled with one of her famous softball-mom whistles. She explained that none of us was in any position to complain, because this was what she was able to find on her first trip and that she had received plenty of cash from the stock certificate to outfit all of us later. We could all feel free to shop for ourselves once we changed into our new clothing.

At that point, Linda noticed the work we had done on the house. She marveled at the sheer tonnage we had removed from all the lower rooms. We explained that we had put the less suspicious materials such as books in the kids' rooms and the dead giveaways like the TV, DVD player, and the computer in the attic. She seemed impressed and maybe even a little pleased. We all changed into our new clothes, which seemed to smell like burlap and were about as comfortable. Sammy was not crazy about wearing a dress, but Linda told her if she would try it, she might find her a pair of bib overalls like Nate had. I sported a nice brown wool suit, a wool long-sleeved shirt, and a black wool hat. Although I was sure Nate would say I looked cool, I sure didn't feel cool. In fact, I was about to insist that we needed to shut the windows and turn on the air when I caught myself.

Abby was a whole other matter. None of us expected Abby to approve of anything Linda could buy for her from a 1909 drygoods store. However, Linda had appealed to Abby's vanity. Abby emerged from her room sporting an honest-to-God smile, or as close to a smile as her pride would allow. Linda had found her a very attractive pink dress, long white gloves, pink hair ribbons and a matching pink parasol. She stepped awkwardly in brand new shoes identical to Linda's that made an even more harsh slapping sound on the oak floorboards. I grinned at her and tried to give her an appreciative hug, but she pushed me away and assured me that she was only going to wear it until she could get downtown and buy something "comfortable." Neither Linda nor I was ready to climb *that* hill with her. Linda did point out that it could be much worse: the only underwear she saw at the dry goods store was made from wool. She had decided to forgo the wool undies as it was 1909 after all and who was going to be inspecting our underwear? I was the only one who noticed that Linda had directed the question to Abby and had uttered it with an emphasis on *underwear*. Not wanting to know what that was about, I ignored it.

Nate, Linda, and Abby headed back downtown for more clothing. I took Sammy for a stroll past Dr. Fischer's house. I still had no clue how we had gotten to 1909 or why it happened, but I felt certain that Dr. Fischer could help us sort it out somehow. When we reached the corner, we turned and continued around the block. It was then I noticed that even the side streets were made of a combination of dirt and brick, making an odd crazy-quilt pattern. The gas streetlights that had been evenly spaced all the way down Main Street to the downtown area were now few and far between. When we reached Linn Street, we turned back west. I was afraid Sammy would notice that her school was gone, but she was too busy trying to keep from stepping on her long dress and getting used to her funny shoes to take any notice of anything else. Two stray dogs stopped briefly to sniff us but ran off before Sammy could introduce herself properly. This gave rise to serious thinking about why Sarge had disappeared and how I was ever going to explain her absence to Sammy.

Back on Main Street, we saw a boy a few years older than Sammy gleefully pushing a steel hoop down the street with a long T-shape stick. Sammy bolted to the street before I could even act. She grabbed the stick from the boy and began rolling the hoop in the opposite direction. The boy once he overcame his surprise, yanked the stick back from Sammy and yelled "Hey stupid! Girls can't do this!" and continued down Main Street in disgust.

I tried to console Sammy, but she was clueless as to why anyone would tell her anything was out of bounds because she was a girl. We were almost home, and I was about to abandon my plan to drop in on Dr. Fischer and just take Sammy in for a cool drink when I looked up and saw Dr. Fischer coming down the walk toward us. I was unsure about what to say, and was thankful that he spoke first. "That boy can be kind of mean," he explained, "but he's a good boy most of the time." When he extended a hand with a dollop of hardened sugar on a stick, I realized he had emerged to comfort Sammy.

"I'm Dr. Silas. What's your name young lady?" he continued.

"Sammy" she answered wide-eyed.

"Sammy's a boy's name, isn't it?" he winked at me.

"My name's Samantha Jo Murphy, but everybody calls me Sammy," she explained.

"Well, I'm gonna have to think on that one a bit *Sammykins*" he offered as he reached out and tickled her chin.

I knew I had to broach the subject of our identities, but I could only get out "Hot enough for ya?" Silas gave me a puzzled look and reminded me it was only 65 degrees.

I finally got up the nerve to ask if Mrs. Clark had recovered from our encounter that morning. He pointed out that she was really a very nice person and very likeable but that we, particularly Linda, had just surprised her. I apologized for Linda although I wasn't completely sure for what, so I kept it brief. He seemed satisfied. But then I just blurted out "Why did you tell Mrs. Clark we were from Indiana?"

His face told me I need not fear anything he was about to say. "Anybody who laid eyes on you could tell you weren't from Marshalltown. I thought it would make all of our lives easier if Mrs. Clark had some facts to consider. She's just a lot easier to live with when she doesn't have to draw her own conclusions. Look, I don't know what you are doing here, but as soon as I saw you this morning, I knew you weren't here to cause any trouble, so I made up that little story to stop Mrs. Clark from wool gathering. I figure you'll tell me what's what when you're ready."

"But what was that part about the McGrews being gone for a year?" I asked.

"They're in Europe on a buying trip, better part of a year," he explained half sounding like he thought

I should know that. I took a minute to mull over what I had just learned and to try to sort out just how much detail I could trust this man with right then. I decided that we couldn't expect anyone to believe the whole thing at once and that if he did turn out to be as nice as he appeared, the rest of it could wait. I opted for a change of subject.

"Sammy, what should you tell Dr. Silas for the candy?"

"Thank you, Dr. Silas" she offered with the wooden stick protruding from her disarming smile as she gave his legs a hug.

"Why don't you go inside and play and I'll be in to read you a book in a bit," I said. Sammy headed on in, stopping briefly to tell Silas "Bye."

"What a sweetie pie," Silas smiled.

"Yeah, she is most of the time. Look, Dr. Fischer, here's the thing. We didn't really want to come here. You could say we just had some bad things happen to us. I really do appreciate what you did for us this morning, and again I apologize for Linda. She's not usually like that. She's actually very level-headed most of the time. She's a nurse you know." That got a raised eyebrow from him. I wasn't sure why, but it seemed like he was filing that tidbit away permanently. "We all have a lot to deal with and we'll probably need some help. It's great to have a neighbor like you to turn to. Have you lived here long?"

"I am from Pennsylvania originally, but I stayed in Marshalltown when I was mustered out of the Army after the War in '66. I was a surgeon during the war. When it ended I just stayed here; I had no reason to return to Pennsylvania . . ." His voice trailed off as he watched Sammy plod up the front walk. I was certain there was more to it than that but just as certain that he had already told me more than he ever intended to.

I tried to grasp the fact that I was standing in the middle of Main Street, posing as a crazy man from Indiana, talking to a Civil War veteran more than 60 years before I was born. Moreover, I was in an itchy wool suit.

Suddenly, Silas regained his thoughts. "So how long do you folks expect to stay?"

"Well, that's hard to say. We need to get back on our feet and get some things together. Our plans are sort of indefinite." I really didn't know what to say.

"Well," he started, placing his hand on my right shoulder as he turned to go home, "you seem like a real nice fella. I hope everything works out for you and your family. I look forward to meeting all of them soon. Good day!" With that, he turned and followed his cane back toward the door of his house.

"Good day to you too, Doctor and thanks again." He gave me a wave over his back .

I went back in the house. It was strange to step inside our house, where it was so much easier to pretend that everything was still *normal*, that we were still the Murphy family of West Main Street in good old 2009. However, all I had to do was look back outside at the people on the street and it was obvious that nothing was normal, at least not for us.

I called for Sammy and heard her small voice coming from her room. I climbed the stairs and found her in her room holding her Barbie doll and looking out the window. From the east window in Sammy's room, we had always had a nice view of the city as far as the trees permitted. Now, I could see the Marshall County Courthouse four blocks away clearly because so few trees were tall enough to block the view. I could also see that Sammy was upset.

"What's the matter, Sammy?" I asked.

"Why didn't that boy like me?"

"Oh, I think he liked you fine. Who wouldn't like you? I think you just surprised him when you tried to play his game." I lied through my teeth; I thought he was a rude brat, but I thought Sammy had enough to deal with without hearing that from me. "Come here." I turned her to me and hoisted her to my knee as I sat on the edge of her bed. "What do you say we read a book until Mom and Nate and Abby come home?"

"OK! Read me <u>Little Red Riding Hood</u>," Sammy begged, somewhat like her old self. She pulled the book out of her book basket and I began to read. Sammy lay down on the chenille bedspread on her "big bed" and continued stroking Barbie's wiry plastic hair. The more I read, the less she moved. After a few pages, I could see a nap coming her way. I closed the book and waited; her eyelids fought off sleep. I tried singing "You Are My Sunshine" quietly like her mother, but my toad-like croaking made her eyes pop wide open. I switched to humming and she settled in again. In a few minutes, she was out like a light.

I slipped back down the stairs to the kitchen thinking I'd try to make a cup of coffee the old-fashioned way. I got as far as the table when I saw the wax-stained package of candles. I opened it and found a dozen long, thick, off-white candles and a skeleton key. I put the candles away in the cupboard and headed for the front door with the key. I tried to insert it in the lock but fumbled just enough that it slipped from my hand and hit the hard oak floor, bounced once, and landed in the entryway floor register. I got down on my knees and fished it out of the register and stood up cracking my head on the doorknob on the way up. The pain was excruciating, but I managed to keep the cursing within the whisper range so as not to wake Sammy. As I sat on the floor leaning against the wall, it suddenly occurred to me: What if the door was somehow responsible for our predicament? What if all we needed to do was to unlock it and return to 2009? What if I had opened it just then? Where would that have left Linda and the kids?

I crawled away from the door a safe distance and got to my feet. I put the key away in the cupboard with the candles and started some water boiling in a pan on the stove while I paced the floor and rubbed my head. I could hear a streetcar coming up Main Street from downtown. I looked out the window just in time to see Nate jump off the moving streetcar with a large package and head up the walk. Once the car stopped, Abby and Linda also got off loaded with packages; I hoped Linda had gotten a *lot* of money from that stock certificate. Nate came up the front steps and rang the doorbell, but I motioned him through the curtained window to go around.

Once they were inside, it was Christmas all over again. These packages held more clothes for all of us, but mainly for the clotheshorse, Abby. Nate made a cute little joke about her wardrobe being "dated" and she smacked him for it. The box Nate had carried held two kerosene lamps, a can of kerosene, and two fine watches, one for Linda and one for me. Linda answered my disapproving look by simply reminding me that at 1909 prices, shopping was like playing store.

According to my new watch, it was 11:30. Because I had skipped breakfast, I suggested we have lunch. Linda went to check on Sammy while I made some sandwiches out of the last of the bread. This reminded me of the grocery-shopping situation, and I wondered exactly when the expression "the greatest thing since sliced bread" came into existence. I was afraid we would find out very soon.

Linda came back downstairs reporting that she thought Sammy could use more sleep, so we gathered around the table to eat without her. Nate was quiet even for him and Abby was giving her cell phone one more try.

"This sucks!" Abby blurted suddenly. "How could this have happened? Why me?"

"None of us likes this, Abby," Linda reminded her. "And we don't have any answers. I just hope that sometime soon, whatever put us here will put us back in 2009 and this will just be a memory."

"A *bad* memory," Nate observed.

This seemed like a good time to pose my questions about the door and the key. I shared that I had almost tried the key in the lock and my reasons for waiting. I left out the part about dropping it and cracking my head on the knob. I explained that if the door was somehow to blame for our jumping back in time, maybe we could use it to return to 2009. I felt that all three of them were mentally sizing the old man up for the rubber room—I was glad I had not mentioned the bump on the head now. Slowly, the looks turned from skeptical to pensive to interested.

Nate spoke first. "You know, Dad might be onto something. We never had this problem before he installed the door. And it did lock by itself when it slammed shut last night around 11."

"Well, any door lock can do that if it's well lubricated like Hank had it," I challenged.

Linda broke a long silence. "It's not any lock, it's the lock that was put in the door when the house was built in 1908. Joe, it wasn't *around 11*; I checked the clock by my bed when it woke me up. It happened, at exactly *midnight*."

Another, longer silence ensued, broken this time by Nate. "Then we've gotta try it. Get the key and try it. I got a game this afternoon at 2!" I looked at Linda and she gave me her "What the heck; go ahead" look.

"Well, not so fast," I cautioned. "Has anyone seen anything of Sarge?" There were dumb looks all around. "I think whatever happened only affected the *inside* of the house. I think we haven't seen Sarge because she was *outside* the house when it happened; she's still in 2009. Any one of us who isn't *inside* the house whenever it happens again might stay in 1909. That's why I waited to try the key until everyone was home."

"OK, Dad, we get it." Nate pleaded. "That makes sense. We're all here now; get that key and let's get out of here. I've got a game and these clothes are killing me." I got a "go ahead" look from Linda, but then she asked me to wait until she could go get Sammy.

I got the key from the cupboard and fought for pole position with Nate and Abby who had already crowded into the entryway. When Linda and Sammy came down the stairs, they joined us in front of the door. I saw that they were just as nervous as I was. My fingers shook as I inserted the key into the lock; then I stopped and asked if we shouldn't say a prayer or something. Everyone assured me that *that* had already happened many times over. They all held hands, and, closing my eyes, I turned the key until I heard the lock make that unmistakable hollow metallic click. I opened my eyes and listened. It was just as quiet outside as it was in the entryway. As I turned the knob, we heard footsteps on the porch. Abby screamed "Jeff?" and threw the door open. A horrified Mrs. Clark screamed and threw a plate of oatmeal cookies into the air and over her shoulder across the front porch. A very disappointed Dr. Fischer stood behind her, shaking his head as cookies rolled off the porch into the dirt.

CHAPTER 4

Any other time, the humor of the situation would have been welcome, but all any of us could manage was half-hearted apologies for scaring the bloomers off Mrs. Clark. The second time. In less than 24 hours. Sammy did offer up a very warm, "Dr. Silas!" as she ran past Mrs. Clark to give him another hug. I tried to help Mrs. Clark to her feet, but I would have stood a better chance of helping her out of the bathtub. Linda apologized again and picked up the cookies from the porch floor, commenting on how delicious they smelled.

Nate and Abby slunk back into the house. We both begged Mrs. Clark and Silas to come in. She would rather have entered a bull pasture wearing her red flannels, but Silas nudged her with his cane adding "Go on woman; we came over to welcome the Murphys to Marshalltown. They mean you no harm." She proceeded hesitatingly and unconvinced, entering our house like a cow prodded to the slaughter on the tip of Silas' cane. Once inside, they both surveyed the interior. He searched for clues of our origins, she for the death traps and torture instruments she was certain awaited her. I steered them into the living room, although Linda referred to it as the "parlor." I offered to get them something to drink. Silas accepted for both of them, but I could see that

Mrs. Clark didn't intend to let anything we offered touch her lips.

When I returned with the drinks, Linda had already made introductions. Silas explained that he had met Sammy and me in the street earlier in the day and that I had explained something of our situation to him. Linda immediately shot me a furrowed brow, but I just smiled back and asked Mrs. Clark if she was feeling any better. Linda thanked her again for the cookies and asked if she would be willing to share her recipe. Mrs. Clark nodded and took a small sip from her glass.

Sammy closed in on Silas and he extended his hands to pick her up and hold her on his lap. "Have you been napping, young lady?" he asked as he stroked her cheek. The pattern of her chenille bedspread still showed clearly on her face. Sammy nodded twice and then asked how he knew. Silas explained that she must have been getting her beauty sleep because she looked even more beautiful than before. This brought a smile to Sammy *and* to Mrs. Clark.

We talked for more than 30 minutes about our family, places where Linda could shop, and the weather. Their questions about the McGrews and our origins I handled, making up answers as I went, hoping that Linda was taking good mental notes so we could keep our stories straight in the future so to speak. By the time they got up to leave, Mrs. Clark had not only smiled but had actually laughed out loud when Silas recapped the events of the cookie incident on our porch. Then Silas surprised all of us by offering to show us around Marshall-town in his Model T Ford. Looking at each other, neither of us coming up with a reason not to, we accepted.

He said he would call for us at 5:30. They headed home nipping at each other like a married couple.

As soon as they had gone, we all reconvened around the kitchen table to discuss what to try next with the door. Nate inspected the key as if hoping to find some magic encryption or maybe a defect to explain why we were still sitting in a Victorian kitchen instead of cheering him from the bleachers of his baseball game. We tried out various explanations for why the key had failed, but hope was starting to sell kind of cheap. We all agreed to try again at midnight since that was when "it" had happen in the first place. However, I sensed that Linda supported the idea with less passion than the rest of us; I knew even without asking her that she did not want to return before we had had a thorough tour of 1909 Marshalltown.

We suggested Nate and Abby take Sammy for a walk in search of a playground or ball field in the neighborhood, and to our surprise, they agreed. As their voices trailed off down the street, we could hear each trying in vain to convince the other that their 1909 life sucked the most. Linda and I racked our brains for explanations as to why it had happened in the first place and ideas for getting back. We were glad to have the time to discuss it without the kids around because our theories were divided between our being sent to 1909 on some grand high mission and our being punished for some terrible thing we had done. Maybe we were supposed to prevent some awful tragedy or change the outcome of some event that had somehow veered off its cosmic trajectory. I considered that someone up there had tired of our obsessive devotion to the restoration, but I kept that thought to myself because I knew it would only hurt Linda. Besides, she had probably already had the same thought. We grasped at straws. Linda finally gave voice to what we both feared the most; "Joe, what if there is no mission or wrong to be righted and this was just it? What if . . . "

"No!" I interrupted. "Don't even think that! There has to be an explanation and once we figure it out, we'll do whatever it takes." I ended my lecture once I realized I was trying to reassure myself as much as Linda. I sat back down at the table across from Linda and held her hand. Tears formed in her big blue eyes as she squeezed my hand tightly.

The kids returned, each with an observation to relate, their apparent excitement inversely related to their age. Abby found very little about 1909 Marshalltown to like; the houses were "sort of cool," but the people they had met were "sweaty and smelly" and there was absolutely nothing to do. Nate took notice of how many buildings that he had been used to seeing didn't exist yet and was shocked to see how small the town actually was. Absolutely nothing existed South of Linn Creek except farms. He had, on the other hand, met a friend. Nate explained that they had met "Georgie," who was by Nate's description an honest to God, 1909 street kid, complete with cigarettes, a slingshot, and foul language. And he liked to play baseball. He called it "stickball," but a rose by any other name….

We discussed the tour that Silas had offered and who would be going. Abby declared, "I'm not! I'll just stay home and watch…" Realizing there not only would be no TV, but that she couldn't call anyone on her cell phone either, she reversed herself. "Oh, what the hell? It might be fun," she said. Nate was all for it because he wanted to see the rest of 1909 Marshalltown. Sammy was willing to go anywhere Silas was going.

We all scrubbed and changed clothes; you would have thought we all had dates to the prom. Dinner was surprisingly calm. Not all of the conversation revolved around our plight or how to escape it. Everyone had something to share about the day. For once, no one had a complaint about the meal, not so much because of the quality of the food, as the relative unimportance it held, given our situation. Linda and I cleared the table and did the dishes while Nate and Abby passed the time staring out the window as if waiting for 2009 to come rolling down the street.

Promptly at 5:30, the faint putt-putt of Silas' Model T and the ah-oo-gah of its horn announced his arrival at the curb. We were surprised to see no sign of Mrs. Clark as we filed out of the house and down the front steps to our waiting carriage. We were also surprised to see that it held so few passengers, which explained Mrs. Clark's absence. Silas had it covered; he offered to take Abby and Nate for a short spin first and then take Linda, Sammy, and me on an actual tour. Seeing no other option, we gave Abby and Nate the lecture about car safety and not distracting Silas. We felt foolish when we realized that even though there were no seat belts or airbags, its top speed was somewhere this side of a mountain bike and it was practically the only car on the road.

Silas returned within 15 minutes with Nate and Abby in about the same condition they had left, plus a little road dirt and minus Abby's hair ribbon. They didn't have much to say, but they looked as if they had seen ghosts. We assumed their solemn looks were related to what they had not seen (the entire southern half of Marshalltown, the Mall, and all their favorite haunts).

As we boarded Silas' pride and joy, Sammy asked matter-of-factly where the "car seat" was. Before Linda or I could think of a response, Silas shot back, "My word child, you're sitting on it. Haven't you ever ridden in a Model T before?" Linda's hand gently covered Sammy's mouth before she could recite the litany we had taught her about why children were never to ride in *anyone's* car *without* a car seat and a securely buckled seat belt. I quickly defended Sammy by pointing out that this was indeed her first ride in a "motor car." Silas gave me the same look of disdain he had given earlier in the day when I had complained about the temperature.

Silas headed east down Main Street toward the center of Marshalltown carefully weaving in and out of the path of the streetcars. Linda had shared precious little about downtown Marshalltown after her brief shopping trip. From our house, we could see the clock tower of the Courthouse over the tops of very young trees. As we closed in on the business district, I could see that there were many teeth missing from the familiar smile of downtown Marshalltown storefronts. Many of the brick buildings looked familiar, but there were so many wood-frame stores that seemed completely out of place. I knew that rot or fire would eventually claim most of them and that familiar brick structures would replace them. As we neared Center Street, we came upon a small hotel, although the building didn't look at all familiar.

Through the window we could see a desk clerk in a white shirt with sleeve garters reaching for a room key for a newly registered guest; a bellhop waited with luggage in hand. Across the street patrons of a cafe were sitting down to a meal. As we passed various points of interest, Silas yelled descriptions over the noise of the motor like some over weight tour guide. Linda and I feigned interest in his commentary, but most of the scenery was all too familiar. The Marshall County Courthouse was the centerpiece of the downtown area, just as we knew it in 2009. We knew it had to be at least 6 P.M. as all the businesses except the taverns and cafes had closed. The few people we saw appeared to be more interested in Silas' vehicle than they were in its occupants; mothers clutched their children's hands and drew them near as we passed. Some of the fathers seemed to stare in awe, perhaps dreaming of owning a car of their own some day. Those in horse-drawn rigs clearly had no use for the Model T.

Silas rounded the corner of Main Street and 1st Avenue and there stood a truly familiar sight—Marshall Implement looked just as it had right up until they tore it down in the 1980s. Other than that, we saw very few familiar structures until we reached the tracks several blocks to the south. As we passed the Pilgrim Hotel on the corner of 3rd Avenue and Main Street, we met up with a line of horse-drawn passenger wagons Silas called "hacks" as he cussed their drivers for assuming they would get any right of way at all from automobiles. They seemed to be taxiing rail passengers from the depot to hotels. Suddenly I realized why we called taxi drivers "hack drivers."

From Madison Street, where the depots and rail yards were located, we could see nothing but farmhouses, barns and cornfields on the southern horizon, but all along the tracks in either direction were the factories and plants that employed the working citizens of Marshalltown. Each of them made its mark on the landscape with towering smokestacks belching acrid smoke into the Marshall County sky. Silas stopped in front of Stones' Restaurant and launched into a history lesson about Henry Anson, who founded Marshalltown in 1854, and a summary of the major industries.

All the while, Linda and I perused the surroundings for the source of the awful smells permeating the evening air. Having eaten at Stone's many times, we were certain they originated somewhere else. It was a mixture of acrid smoke, sour milk and something else. An odor we knew all too well had originated with human beings and seemed to be coming from the recently arrived passenger train standing in the station with steam hissing from under the cars. Yet another olfactory treat greeted us as the breezes shifted from the east. It didn't quite seem like manure although there were plenty of pigpens within nose shot.

As Silas droned on about the city's industries, he pointed out the Lennox factory on the east end of the city and the sawmill and foundry just before that. Finally, he referred to the creamery that was apparently the source of the worst of the choking odors.

"What's the matter, Honey?" Silas begged of Sammy when he finally ran down to the point that he noticed her scrunched up nose. "Oh, that's just the vinegar works," he explained, nodding in the direction of the building across the street from Stones'. "Sort of smells like pickles, doesn't it?"

We chatted politely with Silas, realizing that he was just proud of his Marshalltown and that we really should appear to be impressed although it was difficult not to show our disappointment. Rather than the Victorian grandeur we had expected, we were met with a cavalcade of sights and smells we would be happy to forget. Everywhere we looked the side streets were a mixture of dust, potholes, and mud puddles.

Only the main downtown streets were paved with bricks. Road apples, and other disgusting reminders of what had passed by in the last 24 hours or so, garnished most of the streets. Garbage hung from topless barrels in the alleys, making it look like a busy day at the Iowa State Fair, except we knew no one was coming by in a golf cart to whisk it all away in the next few minutes. The presence of the barrels peppered the air of every alley with a stench somewhere between rotten eggs and eau de landfill. Even in the early evening light, we could see beady little eyes looking up at us from nearly every storm drain and gutter. I felt Linda pressing closer and closer to me the further we drove. When she couldn't stand any more, she cleverly asked to see some of the finer houses of Marshalltown. Looking somewhat miffed, Silas reminded her that the best houses in Marshalltown were on Main Street, the part of Main Street where *he* lived. Nonetheless, he headed the car west on Madison to 13th Street where we turned north.

We expected to see Miller Middle School or Marshalltown High School, but instead we saw what looked to be a dumpsite, the empty lot littered with all manner of trash and cast-off items. As we moved north on 13th I was relieved somehow to see the guard towers at the entrance to the Iowa Soldiers Home come into view. I suppose I took this as proof that we were finally coming to a part of Marshalltown we would recognize, but of course the post-WW II neighborhoods we were so fond of were nowhere to be found.

East of the Soldiers Home were only random shacks and a few tenement buildings all the way down to 6th Street to the east and State Street to the south. No cottages with red-tiled roofs or stucco-covered bungalows with picket fences, only a few small farm buildings in a large open field. Up by the Iowa River between 8th and 9th Streets, the stately houses of the Hughes Grove neighborhood were a pleasant contrast to the simple cookie-cutter bungalows we had seen so far. Before we could ask, Silas explained that dentists, optometrists and pediatricians, most of whom kept office hours and worked out of the Woodbury building downtown, populated this neighborhood (which he referred to as "Pill Hill"). It was obvious from the disgust in his voice that he did not consider them to be real doctors. We simply nodded in agreement and wondered to ourselves what he would make of 21st-century doctors and their technological advances, not to mention their fees. Moreover, medical insurance—well we did not intend to get into that discussion with Silas.

As simple and limited as 1909 Marshalltown was, our tour took almost 45 minutes. By the time, Silas pulled up in front of our house, it was almost 6:30 and we were actually tired, if not from the physical jostling Silas' motorcar gave us on the pothole-filled streets, certainly from the mental strain of keeping up the pretense of being a typical 1909 family.

We thanked him sincerely, telling him what a nice town he had. "Oh, this isn't <u>my</u> town," he explained as he pulled away. "I'm from Pittsburgh. I just stayed in Marshalltown when I mustered out after the War." With that, he tipped his hat to Linda, putt-putted away to his carriage house, and put the Model T away for the night.

"Daddy, was Silas in the "*Vet-Nom*" War?" asked Sammy.

"No he's older than that," I answered.

"Apparently he's a *lot* older than that," Linda added.

CHAPTER 5

We were used to returning home and finding that Abby and Nate had left every light on in the house. However, this evening, when we left, we had no electricity and I suppose neither of us expected our 2009 lights or appliances to work in 1909. Nate had restored our electrical power through a stroke of genius he apparently did not inherit from me; he checked the breaker box and found the main breaker tripped. He had also tinkered with about everything in the house and found that it all functioned well. Freshly washed dishes were drying in the drainer and the kitchen was spotless. Abby addressed our looks of disbelief by explaining, "There wasn't anything *else* to do!"

We compared notes and learned that Nate had indeed found a baseball diamond of sorts behind Arnold School; not the same thing as Little League, but it gave him reason to hope. Abby acted as though she still halfway expected Jeff to pull up outside for his nightly call, although I'm sure she had trouble picturing him behind the wheel of a Model T. "I saw some cute boys," Abby eventually reported, "but they were all so dirty looking and everyone was dressed like they're on the way to church; what's with that?" We told them about the other houses we had seen and about the hotels, horse-drawn hacks, and the fact that we could all still eat at Stone's; we weren't going to mention the vinegar works, but Sammy did it for us. She summed it up nicely with "It smells stinky."

"And so will you, young lady, if we don't get you in the tub," Linda shot back as she reached for and missed Sammy at the start of their nightly bedtime chase. Sammy shrieked with joy as she ran up the stairs with Linda in hot pursuit. Sammy was oblivious of our plight, and for the moment, I envied her. Nate and Abby looked at me as if they expected me to come up with a solution any second. I knew my eyes were giving away what I did not want to put into words; I had no clue why it had happened or when it would be over, or even if we would ever return to our own time. All I really knew for sure was that we didn't belong in 1909 and that I was really starting to despise the Victorian house that we thought we *had* to have.

When we heard Linda's voice softly singing "You Are My Sunshine" to Sammy, we knew it wouldn't be long before she rejoined us and we could try to plot another assault on the time warp that had become our life. Linda soon returned with an idea.

Since the switch had apparently happened when the door blew shut at midnight we decided to wait up until 11:55 and make repeated tries with the door lock until after midnight. Staying awake was no problem for Nate and Abby, but the old folks had to have caffeine. We passed the time by playing cards and telling stories. As the time came, Linda brought Sammy down in her blanket and I repeatedly unlocked and opened the door for nearly 30 minutes, checking each time for signs of the 21st century. However, nothing ever changed; each time

I opened the door, we could see the streetcar tracks in front of our house shining under the light of the street lamp. Finally, at 12:30, we admitted defeat and made the climb up to bed. Nate and Abby soon followed. Although they both swore they weren't tired, within minutes we were all sharing a goodnight that would have made the Waltons proud of us.

∽

For the next few days, we racked our brains about what we could possibly do to resolve our dilemma. We considered variations on the theme: blowing the door shut with a fan, leaving it shut day in and day out until we returned, even a Rube Goldberg type contraption involving a deadfall and levers and ropes that looked like something from a Three Stooges movie. Abby even suggested paying Georgie, $5 to come over at exactly 12 midnight and slam the door shut (from the outside of course). They were certain that for $5, Georgie would do about anything. Obviously, few of our ideas made any real sense and the ones we put into practice did absolutely no good. Unless you want to count the fact that for the first time in a long time, we were working together as a family.

We passed the one-week anniversary of our arrival still squarely in the Victorian Era. Judging from the front page of the newspaper it was just another slow news day for the country. The top national story was about Alice Huyler Ramsey, a 22-year-old housewife and mother from Hackensack, New Jersey, who had become the first woman to drive across the United States. With three female companions (none of whom could drive a car), she drove a Maxwell automobile the 3,800 miles from Manhattan, New York, to San Francisco, California, in only 59 days! Nate was quite amused by this; Abby not so much.

The White House was still occupied by President Taft, and we would all be very old (or dead) before we saw 2009 again the hard way, waiting for time to pass. If we were ever going to get our lives back, it would be up to us to figure out how. I suppose it was at this point that Linda and I began to accept that we were in for a long wait.

One thing we all agreed on was that Dr. Fischer was critical to our survival in 1909; he was not only being very neighborly (in his own way), but he had actually covered for us with Mrs. Clark and seemed to have accepted our fabrications about our origins in all their various forms. One thing was clear; no matter why we were in 1909, we weren't going to be able to leave without getting to know this man a lot better. It was equally clear that like it or not, we would have to win over Mrs. Clark in the process.

Never one to shrink from a challenge, Linda set about winning the old biddy over. She made a call to ask Mrs. Clark for her recipe for oatmeal cookies and returned with just that, the recipe and nothing more. Linda tried to talk to Mrs. Clark while the housekeeper hung her laundry out to dry, but quickly learned not to get in Mrs. Clark's way when she had work to do. Eventually she settled on a strategy Nate called CSU (constantly sucking up). Every time she was near Mrs. Clark, she made at least one compliment about her appearance, her house keeping, her skin, anything. She knew it could be a long up hill battle, but she figured she had plenty of time. Even from the beginning, Linda's tactics showed promise as Mrs. Clark gradually raised fewer and fewer questions about us.

I, on the other hand, concentrated on getting to know Silas as well as possible. So far in the week that we had known him, none of us had been over to his house. It was an unusually large Victorian home with too many rooms for one person. However, I assumed the back half of the home was the domain of Mrs. Clark. The brick structure not only kept Silas in the comforts of the time (parlor with a fireplace, formal dining room, indoor plumbing) but also allowed ample room for his limited medical practice. Silas had to be pushing 70 and showed few signs of slowing down, but it appeared that his practice consisted mainly of treating children of the poor and older people who may have been more comfortable with someone a bit wizened holding the stethoscope. He kept to his home most of the day, so I assumed he didn't have rounds at St. Thomas Hospital and, for that matter, didn't have privileges there either. His fondness for referring to hospitals as "breeding grounds for disease" supported that idea.

The only indication that his home even contained a doctor's office was the small glass sign with gold-leaf lettering "Dr. Silas W. Fischer, M.D." hung inside the window of the parlor. As I came up the walk, I wondered how the elderly patients we had seen coming and going navigated the rather steep steps leading to the porch. Most of them appeared to need treatment for "rheumatism" and I knew that then, as in our time, a doctor's best efforts brought them little relief. I climbed the steps and rang the bell; Mrs. Clark answered the door with a few more degrees of warmth than usual. "Yes, Mr. Murphy, Doctor's in; are you needing medical attention?" she asked somewhat skeptically.

"No, I'm fine thank you. I just wanted to have a few words with him," I explained, hoping that I'd *never* have to explain any ailment to *her*. "If he's busy, I can come back later."

"No, I think he can take time to see you now," she assured me. She led me to a good-sized room across the hall from the parlor, which I was sure would be a study or library, but was actually a well-equipped 1909 medical office. The library shelves contained Silas' medical texts as well as the lighter reading of the day. The furniture included Silas' huge roll-top desk (still closed), an examination table not unlike the one in my uncle's office in the '50s (stirrups and all), a large white wall cabinet with a glass door full of medicines. Across the room was a tall balance beam scale. On a small table next to Silas' desk were a very crude brass microscope, a series of jars with cotton balls, bandages, and two thermometers. Above that hung a simple black picture frame with Silas' medical school diploma. I was just honing in on his diploma when I heard his heavy footsteps approaching in the squeaky hallway outside the door. As the door swung open, Silas greeted me using my first name.

"Now what can I do for you, Joe? Mrs. Clark tells me this isn't a professional call."

"Well," I began, "I wouldn't say that. After all, you are a professional and I am seeking your assistance." When Silas didn't appear the least bit impressed, I continued. "The thing is, you know we're new to town and we really appreciate what you have done to show us around. I just wanted to thank you personally and see if there was anything we could do to return the favor."

"That's not necessary. I was glad to do it. That's what we do here in Marshalltown," he assured me with typical midwestern modesty, offering me a chair. I was not unfamiliar with the game; at least two grateful refusals must follow any offer of kindness before eventual acceptance.

"Well, I think taking you and Mrs. Clark out to dinner is the least we could do," I continued. "That's what *we* do, you know, where *we* come from."

"*Indiana,* isn't it?" Silas asked with a raised eyebrow that made me think we hadn't been as convincing as we thought. "No, really there's no need, I was just being neighborly." He sounded as if I had softened him up a bit. He fiddled with two silver dollars in his hand.

"Well, it would only be neighborly of you to show us at least one of the finer dining establishments of the city. Knowing where to dine in a place the size of Marshalltown is important. You show us where and I'll pick up the check." I was confident that I had clinched it.

A slight smile broke his lips. "Well, it would only be right to get you to sample some of Stones' homemade pies." He almost smacked his lips. Shutting the door and lowering his voice, he continued. "Don't you dare tell her, but Mrs. Clark's baking leaves a bit to be desired." He paused and returned the silver dollar to his vest pocket. Then, leaning forward, extending his hand, he offered, "You let me pay for dessert and we've got a deal!" I shook his hand and we both smiled as if closing on a parcel of farmland or maybe a team of horses. I just hoped he wouldn't expect me to smoke a cigar.

"Well, when can we go?" I asked. "How about tonight?"

"Can't. I promised to go with Mrs. Clark to hear Billy Sunday. She thinks *he's* got the cure for what ails *me*!" he bellowed at his own joke. "The woman is death on liquor. It's not as if she has to drag me out of the gutter or sober me up in the morning, for God's sake. I just like a shot of brandy before bed. Helps me sleep."

"And Mrs. Clark objects to that?"

"Gives me fits about it whenever she catches me. I have to wait until she goes to her quarters for the evening in *my own house*! Says it's because she's concerned about my *spiritual* health. She's been after me ever since she joined up the last time he was in town."

"This Sunday fellow, you mean?" I clarified.

"Damn right," he shot back. "Nobody can kill a good time quite like a reformed sinner!" he laughed sarcastically.

"So what's the story on him?" I asked, guessing I already knew the answer.

"Well, he came from these parts and was a pretty fair baseball player for his time. Cap Anson got him to play for Chicago. Damn fast base runner, but his bat was a little sleepy; couldn't hit to save his soul," Silas went on unaware of his own pun. "I'm surprised you haven't heard of him; don't you follow the great American pastime?" Silas gouged, pretending to swing a bat.

"Sure I've heard of Billy Sunday the evangelist. I just didn't realize he had been a baseball player. How'd he get into the religion business?"

"Well, besides loving baseball, he was even fonder of the booze. Seems he came upon a revival meeting when he was three sheets to the wind. After hearing those evangelists belting out familiar tunes, he stepped forward and found the Lord. Worked for one of them for a few years and 'learned the business,' as they say. Then he branched out on his own. Haven't you ever heard him preach?"

"No, he's never been anywhere close to where we lived. I always wanted to," I tried to invent an interest. What an opportunity! I could hear Billy Sunday speak in person-in 1909!

"Well, then now's the time. He's been here most of the spring already. Let's plan on catching his act. Better yet, why don't you go tonight with Mrs. Clark and I'll go to Stones' and have pie!" laughing at his own joke.

I laughed with him once because the thought *was* hilarious and once more so that *he knew* that *I knew* he was joking. I really was curious to hear Billy Sunday, but a date with Mrs. Clark, no way! "I doubt Linda would approve. Let me get back to you."

Just then, Mrs. Clark knocked and entered. "Mrs. Reilly's here. Says she has a stomach problem *again.* Can you see her now?"

"I'll go. I don't want to get in the way of your patients," I offered and stood and moved toward the door.

"Nonsense, Joe," Silas insisted. "What's ailing her 'stomach' isn't going to go away for at least seven to eight months. Poor woman's got five kids to feed now."

I bid Silas and Mrs. Clark farewell anyway. Silas told me not to be a stranger and to drop in anytime. As I was going down the hall, he added, "Come back again and we'll talk some more about *Indiana*," followed by more laughter.

As I headed down his steps, I congratulated myself on how well I had done—I had definitely loosened him up. I had also gotten us a dinner engagement (although we hadn't actually decided on when). I just needed to catch Linda up a bit and prepare her for an evening with Billy Sunday and Mrs. C. Not bad for one morning.

Now if I only I had a clue about why Silas wanted to talk about Indiana and more important what I was supposed to say, since I had never been there.

CHAPTER 6

Just as had I suspected, Linda was less than excited about a church date with Mrs. C. We had both been a little on the outs with God ever since we lost the baby. We weren't entirely sure that there was a God and if there was one, whether He was to blame for this little time-travel practical joke we were living out, but we had more than enough anger about the whole thing to spare a little in His direction. But, on the other hand, for all we knew, Billy Sunday was somehow related to why we had been thrust back to 1909, so ultimately we decided to go have a look. It *was* the last night of the Revival. Besides, with a good Irish name like Murphy, we thought it wouldn't be too hard to convince Mrs. C that we already had religion, although the great Billy Sunday might take a bit more convincing. We decided to go and sit in the back, the far back, maybe near the exit.

The revival was to start promptly at 7 and we expected it to be standing room only so we made it a point to arrive early. Standing room only was certainly believable, as from our house we could see the crowd starting to gather around 5. By the time we started out, the throng of buggies, hacks, and automobiles stretched past our house all the way to 9th Street and just as far to the east. Our little sidewalk group grew quickly as more and more people seemed to just appear from the various forms of transportation. Marshalltown's finest attempted to direct traffic, and volunteers tried to organize the parking, but all in all, it was a grand mess. Streetcars parked for the duration in front of the Tabernacle formed a train of sorts, with an odd assortment of vehicles parked on the tracks ahead of and behind the streetcars.

Pushcart vendors sold everything from popcorn to drinks. Gathered around the base of almost every large tree was a group of men in white shirts, coats over their arms or shoulders, having the last few drags on their smoke of choice. Behind carriage houses, streetcars, or other convenient shelters, dozens of men were swearing off "demon rum" (after one last drink, of course).

As Silas and Mrs. C led the way to the Tabernacle on the corner of Third and Main Streets, we came to a building that seemed to stretch forever. The temporary-looking structure stood on the same spot where we were used to seeing the Central Christian Church. Fully a city block in length, it had the appearance of a huge wooden tent with several doors but almost no windows; the outside looked neither churchlike nor permanent.

The crowd began spilling out the main entrance almost as soon as we arrived. A series of huge wooden posts supported the entire structure; cross-braced at the top, they connected to a network of beams and rafters. The builders had left amazingly few impediments to block a clear view of the stage, which stood at the midpoint of the building, forming a sort of crude religious theater-in-the-round. Huge electrical lights rigged to the poles illuminated the structure; another bank of lights lit the stage. Everywhere we looked, we saw row after row after row of pine benches. According to Silas, volunteers built the entire structure from scratch in less than a month.

Once inside, we were among the last people to find seating. Although the early June heat was still not everything Iowa could throw at us, the humidity was high and moving air was hard to come by. Large fans did little more than make noise; the lucky ones scored one of the paper fans handed out at the door by the local funeral homes. We were not so lucky.

As though added to the hot, humid soup that passed for air just to give it flavor was a mixture of aromas—freshly laundered and starched Sunday-best clothing and 12-hour perspiration undaunted by deodorant with a faint twist of roses from the floral arrangements on either side of the stage. In our little corner of the world, the odor of camphor emanated from a very large woman with an apparent summer cold.

By 6:55, the pianist started repeating his repertoire of hymns. At 7 sharp, a very large round man in a white shirt, black trousers, and suspenders came on stage; Mrs. C told us he was Homer Rodeheaver, Mr. Sunday's chief assistant. He welcomed us to the "87th and final session of the Billy Sunday Sawdust Trail Revival." Sawdust (as well as chewing gum, partially smoked cigarettes, crumpled fans, and old revival programs) covered the center aisle leading from the entrance at the back of the Tabernacle all the way to the stage at the front.

After laying a few ground rules and pointing out "the facilities," Mr. Rodeheaver introduced Billy Sunday to thunderous applause. The crowd rose to their feet in a show of appreciation similar to what I had seen at a modern day rock concert except they held Bibles and hymnals instead of lighters and beer cans. I was pretty sure no one in the crowd had been smoking weed.

Mr. Sunday, a short, stocky man in his late forties, scurried to the center of the stage like a tap dancer in a gray wool suit and immediately took control of the proceedings. After he thanked the crowd and asked that they take their seats, he thanked them again for the tremendous support they had given the revival and announced the totals so far: Previous attendance had totaled 193,800; tonight's attendance was estimated at 5,500, and total conversions so far were 1,762. Impressive stats for a town that numbered 13,500 souls on a good day. Another round of thunderous applause followed this information. After a look in his direction, Mr. B.D. Ackley played the introduction to "Are You Washed in the Blood?" Then the Rev. Sunday asked us to join in singing.

The crowd rose to their feet and gave me a new understanding of the word "tumultuous"; thousands of men, women, and even children were singing in reasonably close harmony, most without the aid of a hymnal. Although the Tabernacle had the acoustics of a hay barn, and there was no amplification, the crowd of worshipers sent forth a sound that I am sure resounded all the way to the Courthouse.

Silas belted out his best nasal tenor rendition and Mrs. C joined in with what must have been a beautiful alto voice years earlier. Linda was even trying to pass as a singer and shot me looks to do the same, although neither of us had heard the hymn before and had no hymnal within reach. We did our best to make sounds on key even if we weren't actually forming words (sort of like patients emerging from a coma). At the conclusion of the hymn, the Rev. Sunday motioned for us to take our places and waited as over 5,000 worshipers took refuge on the pine benches and chairs they could find or stood in the side aisles and at the front and back of the Tabernacle.

Then, before our eyes, as he launched into his final sermon of the Revival, the preacher transformed into the human dynamo that was the Reverend Billy Sunday. Taking no prisoners, he lashed out at the entire liquor establishment, those who manufactured, transported, or sold it but in particular at those who consumed it. Racing from one side of the stage to the other, he punctuated every major point he made with exaggerated facial expressions and physical gestures. Borrowing from his baseball days, he assumed nearly every imaginable pose one might see at the ballpark—including sliding into home plate—all of them crowd-pleasers.

I began to wonder how many had come for the religion and how many just to get a final glimpse of Billy Sunday the former Marshalltown ballplayer turned Chicago White Stocking. It didn't seem to matter much; he had the attention of everyone in the Tabernacle and he was leading them all down the Sawdust Trail toward redemption, some more willingly than others. I noticed Mrs. C shooting looks up at Silas each time the reverend referred to liquor or tobacco. Silas did his best to ignore her, but he had way more sweat on his brow than the actual climatic conditions called for.

Among the standing were clearly those who had come strictly as spectators—newspapermen from all over Iowa and the skeptics who had purposely positioned themselves in the back near the exits. As I looked around at the crowd in our end of the Tabernacle, I noticed that Rev. Sunday's words were affecting people in very different ways. Some were nodding in agreement, even punctuating his major points with "Amen," or "Yes, brother!" somewhat quietly to themselves. Most of these folks were smiling, well dressed, and appeared to be enjoying themselves.

Others, mostly men dressed far less formally, were not smiling but casting downward glances, and a few appeared to wipe an occasional tear. Still others turned to look into the eyes of their spouses or family members and appeared more *worried* than anything; Mrs. C fell into this group. I also realized that a few were just looking around curiously at strangers in the crowd. When my eyes met those of a woman doing the same thing, I returned to studying the program and examining the dirt floor. I realized I had that same feeling I used to get when my grandmother dragged me off to her church and I couldn't wait to get out of it at the conclusion of the services. It was a combination of several discomforts, the heat, feeling *held* against my will, forced to feign allegiance to an unfamiliar theology, and an occasional twinge of guilt as the minister hit a nerve. Only, now I thought it was the heat. Mostly.

Billy Sunday divided his preaching into segments, inserting hymns sung by the choir (numbering in the hundreds) and even a trombone solo by Mr. Rodeheaver. He invited the worshipers to join in on "*Since the Fullness of His Love Came In*" and "*Praise Him, Praise Him*," and they produced sounds not so much polished as sincere, that reached farther and farther down the streets of Marshalltown.

The Rev. Sunday's Sawdust Trail Revival was clearly living up to its reputation. I couldn't make up my mind whether I was more awestruck by his words or by the reality of the moment. The fact that the Rev. Sunday had been dead for over 70 years didn't keep me from hanging on his every word or even from being swayed however slightly by his forceful and convincing portrayal of The Word. Nor was I the least bit put off by the fact that Linda and I were in the company of two people, no, make that thousands of people, who had been dead since long before either of us was born. For the moment at least, that simply did not matter. I was sure that Linda's thoughts somehow aligned perfectly with mine when she gave my hand a squeeze and scooted over closer to me on our bench. As the choir sang "'*Tis So Sweet to Trust in Jesus*," Mr. Rodeheaver asked the ushers to make their rounds with the collection baskets and asked that the crowd contribute generously for the final meeting of the revival.

Near the conclusion of the service, the Rev. Sunday challenged the worshipers to cast aside their sinful ways and to give their life to Christ. He then made the final call for those who were ready to accept Christ into their lives. After a long prayer, the Rev. Sunday, eyes closed, beads of sweat forming on his forehead, began making beckoning motions as Mr. Ackley played chorus after chorus of "*I Love to Tell the Story*." From every part of the Tabernacle, the soon-to-be converted rose from their seats and made the trek down the Sawdust Trail toward the stage. One by one, they took their turn with the Rev. Sunday, praying quietly and sharing words known only to the two of them and to God. After only a few moments with the reverend, they rose quietly and left the stage area, most returning to their seats. A few, overcome by either the heat or the experience or both, required the assistance of the revival workers or family members. No one could have witnessed this process without feeling changed in some way by it.

As the last of those wishing to meet with Rev. Sunday made their way to the stage, Mr. Rodeheaver thanked the crowd again for coming, gave a blessing and declared the meeting to be at an end. Inviting anyone who wished to stay after and meet privately with Mr. Sunday or his staff to do so, he directed Mr. Ackley and the choir into their final number, "*Take the Name of Jesus with You.*" As the crowd began to thin out, ushers made their way down the aisles one more time with the long-handled collection baskets.

We helped Silas and Mrs. C to their feet, both having sat on the pine benches much longer than their arthritis would have advised. We steadied them as they walked on the sawdust-strewn aisle, but once they reached the sidewalk, they both insisted on moving under their own power and guidance. We walked in silence to the corner, where the din of the crowd and the vehicles diminished enough that we could hear each other.

Linda was the first to speak. "Well, I enjoyed the Rev. Sunday's sermon very much!" Linda finally said. "Thank you for inviting Joe and me."

Looking up at Silas, Mrs. C blurted out, "He was talking to you, you know! His warnings about the evils of liquor, those were for <u>you</u>!" she scolded as she clung to his left arm, catching him off guard.

"My God, woman, there must have been over 5,000 people in there. He wasn't talking to me any more than any other man in there who enjoys a good snort once in a while."

"I just thought he made some good points about how we all try too hard to make sense of the Bible. I hadn't thought of it that way before," Linda continued, trying to take the heat off Silas. "How did he put it? 'You might as well try to reason a boil off the back of your neck as to try to reason yourself into religion.' I thought that made a lot of sense."

"So did I!" Mrs. C agreed. "That's what I've been telling Silas for years."

I wanted to spare Silas and get us off the topic entirely by suggesting we all go out for coffee and pie, but I realized with the huge crowd in town, even if there was a restaurant or cafe open on Sunday night, we'd never get in. Thinking better of it, I suggested that we retire to our porch for some lemonade and cookies. Linda immediately shot me that "*How dare you invite company without asking me first?*" look, but I pressed on. "It's starting to cool off a bit, the mosquitoes aren't too bad yet and the company's good. Stop over and sit for a while on our porch."

"On one condition," Silas answered for both of them. "You have to let me stop by my house for some stogies and a bottle of brandy first." With that, he quickly side-stepped Mrs. C's swinging purse and let out one of his trademark bellows.

As we came within sight of our house, Linda excused herself and shot ahead of us, I assumed to do some "straightening up" of the house before we arrived. I dusted off the seats of our porch furniture, but Silas made a beeline for the porch swing and Mrs. C joined him.

"Beautiful evening," I pointed out. Silas and Mrs. C nodded in agreement. I sensed they had a few things to work out, so I excused myself and went inside to assist Linda.

"Well, Martha Stewart, what do you suggest I serve our guests? The only baked goods I have in the house are some Oreo cookies. The closest thing to lemonade I have is some frozen mix. Nice work, Joe!"

Linda was right to be concerned, but I pointed out that it was too dark on the porch for Silas or Mrs. C to notice the print on the Oreos, so we could just explain that you made them with a special press your grandmother brought over from France. If we water down the frozen lemonade a bit, it would probably seem like the real thing.

"Great idea!" Linda shot back. "I'll keep them entertained while you get things ready!" With that, she marched out the front door on to the porch. I knew I had done the only thing worse than putting Linda in the domestic goddess dilemma in the first place: I had found a *simple, guy-type* solution.

The cookies and lemonade were a hit. And just as I predicted, neither of our guests took note of the print on the cookies in the dark of the porch, although Mrs. C did ask how Linda got them to come out so perfectly round. Linda explained with a tone of pride that I was responsible for these cookies and left it at that, knowing that Mrs. C was not at all likely to ask a *man* for cookie-making advice.

Forgetting her anger long enough to recall the original objective for the evening, Linda started the conversation off. "So Silas, what brought you to Iowa?" Linda probed. Seeing that she was doing fine, I just watched and learned, keeping an eye on Mrs. C.

"Well, I guess I got swept up in it, just like everyone else," Silas answered, his mouth full of Oreo. "The War," he explained, seeing our puzzled looks. "When it started I thought it was my *patriotic duty* to go off and tend the wounded and all that. Damn few of them I saved though. Wound up sawing off arms and legs instead."

"How awful!" Linda continued. "But I guess you've dealt with a lot of suffering in your practice over the years."

"Nothing that came close to the War! We had no supplies from the start and it only got worse as the War dragged on. Didn't even have clean water. Infections killed more than the rifles."

"So how did you come to be in Marshalltown?" Linda continued.

"I started out with a Pennsylvania unit, but after Gettysburg, there weren't enough of them left to even count." I worked my way southward with another unit and eventually hooked up with a group of mainly Iowa boys, most of them from this part of the state. When the War ended, I had no particular reason to return to Pennsylvania, so I just settled here and continued doctoring," he explained.

"What about your family?" Linda pried, "Didn't you want to return to them?"

"That's enough talk about the War," Silas snapped. "I came over here to enjoy what's left of the evening."

Comments about what a nice evening it was and how the mosquitoes weren't bad yet ended the long pause that followed. Finally, Mrs. C took the floor. "So Linda, where are you folks from?"

"Indiana!" Linda replied almost indignantly. "Just like we said!"

"So your families are from Indiana?"

"Oh, no," I answered, digging us in deeper. "My parents were from Nebraska, but Dad moved back to Indiana." I paused. "To run his father's business."

"What sort of business?" Mrs. C probed.

"Yes, tell them about your Dad's business—in Indiana," Linda dared, handing me an even bigger shovel.

"Well, it was nothing very interesting really, just paper and supplies—business supplies."

"Oh! My husband was a banker here in Marshalltown; he probably did business with your company. What was the name of your father's business?"

"Murphy Paper!" I blurted with almost scary ease.

"So is that your line of work too?" Mrs. C followed. Having had enough fun at my expense and seeing that the Mrs. C's questions might just paint us both into a bad corner, Linda came to the rescue.

"Actually, Joe was a high school teacher and I was a nurse," Linda explained in a sudden burst of candor. "But we came here to make a fresh start. Joe was tired of teaching and starving, and well, when he inherited a bit of money from his uncle, we decided this would be a good time to get a new start. Joe is going to look into starting a business here in Marshalltown, and I'm going to keep house and care for our family."

I gave her a look that could have wiped out an entire neighborhood. Where had all this come from? She had apparently been thinking about this for a while! How did she think we were going to live even in 1909 unless one of us had a paying job?

"So you've had nurses' training. But surely you don't intend to work now?" Silas probed.

"Well, not for the time being. Unless something comes up where there's a real need. Or the right situation, right Joe?" I was barely able to manage a grunt of agreement, so great was my disbelief.

"You are a very lucky man, Joe," Silas observed as he helped Mrs. C to her feet. "I think you'll like Marshalltown. How long before you plan to get a place of your own?" he asked almost rhetorically.

"Oh, who knows?" Linda sidestepped. "We have so many other things to settle first; we may not even be staying in Marshalltown unless Joe can get a business started."

"Well, we certainly hope you decide to stay," Silas continued. "Mrs. C, I think it's about time I walked you home and let these fine folks get to bed. Thanks for the lemonade, and the cookies were heavenly."

"And thank you for taking us to the Revival," I inserted, finally able to form complete thoughts again. "We both enjoyed it very much and came away with a wonderful message. We enjoyed your company and look forward to doing this again soon."

I helped them down the steps, guided them to the sidewalk, and headed them in the direction of Silas' house before saying goodnight one last time. Then I made a beeline directly for the kitchen, where I expected to find a contrite Linda pleading for forgiveness or maybe even ready to plead insanity, but instead I found the glasses and cookie plate in the sink. That and a brief note which made way too much sense.

> *Joe, what do we have to lose? Besides, you always said I could quit work if it weren't for the mortgage payments. Well, I don't think the next one will be due for about 100 years! Come on up to bed tiger and let's* **discuss** *it!*

As I raced up the steps, I could hear Linda in Sammy's room winding her music box and the first few notes of "Sunshine," lulling her back to sleep after Linda's goodnight kiss. Abby and Nate told me goodnight as I passed their rooms in tones much less sullen than I expected. Linda came silently into our bedroom and without so much as a word, slipped into bed and snuggled up next to me. Silas was spot on—I *was* a lucky man and I had a wonderful family. Now all I had to do was find a way to support them for the next 100 years or so.

CHAPTER 7

As always, Linda was right. It was time that we filled in some of the missing facts from our new persona. It was only a matter of time before Silas and Mrs. C would have pressed us for the finer details of our lives. And they would continue to do so; after all, Marshalltown was a small town and it was important for the residents to know their neighbor's business. We needed to come up with some believable means of support. Linda's stock certificates wouldn't pay the bills forever. Like it or not, it was time for me to find a job.

The newspaper was no particular help in finding work; most of the classifieds were ads for businesses offering to buy or sell something. Had I been looking to sell hides or pelts I would have apparently done well to see H. Willard & Sons of 14 S. 1st Street or if I was looking to buy "dry goods," I should have gone to Nettie

Ingledue and Company of 16 E. Main Street. However, I was looking for a job, and if the newspaper was any indication, I'd be at it a while.

I kissed Linda goodbye and caught the next street-car downtown. Marshalltown's 1909 business district was surprisingly similar to its 21st-century successor, at least Main Street was. Of course, the names on the store-fronts had changed, but many of the buildings I walked past as I trod Main Street in search of work looked very familiar, particularly their upper stories. Little wonder; the plates on most indicated construction dates in the later part of the 19th century. Many of the stores had "Help Wanted" signs in the windows, but everything I inquired about involved menial work such as washing dishes or butchering chickens or hauling garbage out to farmers for their pigs.

Batesole Grocery and D.S. Good Grocery on the south side of Main Street and Reynolds and Sheldon Grocery on the north side were both looking for stock boys, but paid far less than $1.00 a day. F.M Pepper Meats was looking for a meat cutter, but only one with experi-ence. I doubted my years of cutting my own grilled steak would impress them much. I stopped in at C.F. Schmidt Hardware and made my best case as a hardware man, but no sale. It was the same thing at Abbott and Son Hardware.

After a while, I gave up responding to the signs and just walked, taking in the sights and trying to imagine how I, a foreigner in my own town, could possibly fit in to its 1909 workforce. I took stock of my few talents. Ob-viously, I had carpentry skills, but I was totally dependent on power tools that wouldn't be available for at least 50

years, and I wasn't getting any younger. I had seen carpenters working on a new house as I rode the streetcar
downtown, and nothing they were doing looked at all
inviting. Partly because of the hard physical work and
partly because I believed the house I had worked on for
the last few years was to blame for the mess we were in.

I felt I had to be able to find work—I was a college
graduate for Christ's sake! I had paid my way through
college working as a mortician's assistant, but I swore I
would never return to that racket once I graduated. And
graduate I did with a degree in *Psychology*! Thank God,
I was good with my hands! Might as well have been in
arrow-smithing for all the good that would do me now!

As I stopped at the corner of 1st Avenue and Main
Street, debating which way to go next, a horse-drawn
wagon careened around the corner and spilled a portion of its load of construction lumber at my feet. I started to cuss out the driver, but something told me to help
him pick up his boards instead. Working together, we
had most of the load back onto his wagon in less than
five minutes, but I couldn't help noticing that the 2 x 4s
were wider and thicker than their 21st-century cousins. I
tried to make conversation with the man as we cleaned
up the spill.

"I see you're in quite the hurry," I observed brilliantly. I couldn't have impressed him less if I had pointed
out that the sun usually shone during the daytime. I decided to concentrate on the basics. "So do you want the
Douglas fir separated from the cedar or does it matter
to your customer?"

"Hell yes, it matters," he snarled back. "They're for
different orders."

"That's what I figured," I continued. "I know you're pressed for time, but if you have some rope, I could help you tie the load down."

"Grab that hank under the seat then and let's get this done. I got 10 more deliveries to make today and nobody's minding the yard."

I sensed an opportunity. "So you're short-handed? What do you need, an office clerk or a yard man?"

He stopped short and looked me straight in the eye. "Mister, I appreciate your help, but why you so interested in my business affairs?" he asked with a cautious tone.

"Well, it seems like you're doing very well, but you could use some help and I'm looking for a job," I replied. "My name's Murphy. Joe Murphy!" I offered my hand.

His nervous eyes studied me for just a minute and then a slight smile parted his lips as he offered his hand but then retrieved it briefly to remove the sweat-stained work glove. "Name's Wilson, Fred Wilson, owner of Citizen's Lumber. What do you know about the lumber business?"

"I know my way around all the basic building materials. I've repaired houses. I'm familiar with construction techniques." I know my Sunday school teacher would have preferred I stop there, but I added, "And I managed my father's office supply business out in Indiana for the last ten years. All paper is, is wood with an education, right?" He sat down on the tailgate of the wagon and had a small chuckle. I knew I had him.

"I need somebody who's good with figures and can also measure, cut, and load out lumber."

"I'm all that and more!" I could see he was thinking about it. We discussed the details—low pay and only a few days a week to start but it was enough to put food on the table. When he asked how soon I could start, I told him I thought I already had.

I helped him pick up and sort the remaining boards. He wanted me to make the deliveries while he walked back to tend the yard, but I convinced him that I would need a few days to get to know my way around (not to mention learning to drive a team of horses). He drove and pointed out the main intersections as we made our way to the first stop, a house on State Street in need of a new porch. The second half of the load went for a farmer's horse fence. We were back to the yard by 9:30.

Fred gave me the 5-cent tour of his business, ending with a quick trip through the ledger. He was careful not to show me the safe or the balance sheets. Finally he laid down his rules: no credit to anyone without *his* prior approval; any merchandise I needed for personal use was to be paid for just like any other customer (minus my 5 percent discount of course); and absolutely no smoking anywhere on the property! I'd be paid in cash, nothing would be withheld (the IRS was still a few years off), and best of all I wouldn't have to grade papers or deal with other people's children. Yes, it had real promise!

I returned home late in the afternoon expecting praise for finding gainful employment. As I approached the house, I could see Linda and the kids, four of them actually, out on the front step enjoying lemonade in the shade.

"How did it go?" Linda asked when she looked up. I gave her the thumbs-up sign and started to tell her about my good luck, but before I could actually speak, she interrupted, "Oh, Joe, we want you to meet Georgie. He came home from the ball field with Nate."

"Pleased to meet you Georgie," I replied, extending a dirt-covered hand to him. "Do you have a last name?"

"Yes, but everybody just calls me Georgie."

I retrieved my hand with even more filth on it thanks to Georgie. He was pretty much Pig Pen on steroids. Then I noticed his stick and wheel leaning against the step and realized he was the kid Sammy and I had encountered on Day One. He read my disgusted expression as I retrieved my hand.

"Sorry about that. Seems like my hands is always covered with shit!" he apologized. Sammy's eyes widened and her mouth opened as she shot first Linda and then me a look.

"Georgie, I think you mean that your hands are covered with *dirt*," Linda corrected. "Remember what I said about watching your language?"

"Well, it don't matter; eadder way you know what I mean!" Georgie argued. With that, he handed his empty glass back to Linda without a "thank you" and picked up Nate's glove, slipping it on the wrong hand. "Come on, Nate, let's play some more catch!"

"Georgie, you put the glove on the wrong hand. You need a left-handed glove," Nate corrected, looking at me for help.

"You kids have fun and be home in time for supper," I offered, taking the coward's way out.

As Abby followed the two boys down the sidewalk toward the ball lot, I explained my new fully employed status to Linda. She was excited for me, but she seemed to be holding something back. "What's the matter? Aren't you glad I can earn us some spendable money?"

"Yes, I'm happy about that and I know we need the money, but I…, well I don't know…I just hate to see us putting down roots. It makes it seem even more like this will be permanent. And, I've kind of gotten used to having you around in the summer to help with the kids." I was sure there was something else she wasn't telling me, but I didn't think it would accomplish anything to press her for it then.

"Well, I don't know if you've noticed or not, but compared to 2009, I really don't think that the kids need so much supervision. I mean, what harm is going to come to them? All three of them are smart enough to move out of the way of a streetcar most of the time. And Silas and Mrs. C watch Sammy like hawks!" When I turned my back, Linda was gone. I followed her in the house pleading to her to come back so I could finish bragging about my new job, but as I saw her scurry up the stairs, all she offered was "I have to pee…lemonade goes right through me!"

"Mommy has to pee *a lot*!" Sammy whispered. I started to correct her but thought better of it as she scampered up to her room for her doll.

Minutes later, they both came down with the doll and two books. Linda looked tired, so I talked Sammy into "reading" the books to her doll so Linda and I could talk.

"OK, so it's not an impressive job, but it will get us by," I started.

"Yes, Joe, thanks for getting it," Linda assured me as she tugged on my shoulder so she could give me one of her trademarked pecks on the cheek. "I'm sorry I didn't give you my undivided when you got home, but Nate and Abby brought that Georgie kid home, and isn't he a case? I don't think he got all of that dirt playing stickball, at least not today," Linda started.

"Yeah, what's with him? He's the one who was so rude to Sammy the first day we were here. What the Hell is his mother thinking letting him run all over town in those filthy clothes," Linda's look stopped me from ranting on.

"I don't think he has a mother. He said he and his dad live down by the creek on 6th Street. There's nothing down there but shacks and hobo towns. He's a street kid, Joe!"

I mulled that over a bit and then asked, "So are you planning on taking him on or something?"

"I don't know," Linda whined in that way that always told me that, come hell or high water, the stray would be kenneling-up at our house unless I put my foot down. "I know we don't need something else to deal with, but something tells me he needs help."

I had always thought Linda would have made a fine social worker had she not become a school nurse. "What do you mean, Linda? Are you thinking of getting some help for his family or what?"

"No, I wouldn't even know where to begin on that; maybe Silas or Mrs. C would. I just think something is gnawing at him," Linda explained. "I can't put my finger on it, but something's wrong. Maybe that's why we were sent here?"

"To bathe poor kids who live in shacks?" I challenged.

"No, but maybe to try to improve their lot, or I don't know, maybe to save this one kid from his misery or something," Linda offered.

"Come on, let's go rescue our own daughter and read her those books before she makes her poor doll permanently dyslexic," I challenged.

"You two go ahead. I need to lie down for a while." Linda headed into the parlor and talked Sammy into giving up her perch on the couch by offering that I would read to her. I took Sammy and her doll out to the porch swing and checked that Mrs. C wasn't within earshot; I was pretty sure that 1909 Marshalltown wasn't ready for My Little Pony. As I read to my Sammy in the swing, I wondered what Linda was up to now. How many more jobs I would have to take to finance it?

CHAPTER 8

Monday, July 8, 1909

BASEBALL AT NIGHT-Grand Rapids

Defeats Zanesville 11 to 10

As the weeks passed we slowly adapted to 1909. The summer was typical of Iowa with warm temps and breezes, but the real heat came one afternoon in July!

I think we just got too comfortable with Silas and Mrs. C. I will always blame Mrs. C, but for whatever reasons, Silas and Mrs. C began asking more and more questions about our backgrounds in Indiana and Mrs. C in particular became fond of quizzing each of us separately about our relationship to the McGrews; Were they *my* cousins or Linda's? When did we expect them back?

However, everything came to a head on July 28 when Silas dropped in for a visit by himself. He was somber and to the point—eventually.

"Have a seat, Silas. Can we get you anything? Lemonade? Cookies?" I started nervously.

"Maybe some of those nice chocolate cookies with the white filling," he replied with more than a little interest. Linda explained that the kids had finished them off and that she simply hadn't had time to make another batch. She returned with the lemonade and we all three sat around the big oak table in the dining room.

Silas just sat staring at us and sipping his lemonade. He looked at a folded yellow piece of paper in his hand, frowned, and then smiled slightly and then frowned again. He looked around the room as if trying to find some piece of evidence to tell him where to start his interrogation. Finally he spoke. "Joe. Linda. You know that Mrs. Clark and I both think the world of you, but I gotta say your story doesn't add up."

"I can explain," I started, but Linda's grasp of my hand stopped me.

"Our *story*? What *story*, Silas? What part of *our story* needs clarification?" she challenged.

I pulled back. As it was obvious to me that she was at least causing him to feel guilty (one of her specialties), maybe even causing him to *doubt* his doubts. Another interminable silence followed during which he fondled his silver dollar and then returned it to his vest pocket.

When he did speak, it was on a different tack. "I don't know, Linda. I mean you just showed up here without any notice from the McGrews. When Mrs. Clark pressed you for details as to your origin and I offered Indiana, to get her off your backs, you went along with that like you wanted us to believe that you were just dropped here by crows or something. Now today, this telegram comes for Mrs. Clark from the McGrews." He handed us a half sheet of poorly typed text with a Western Union header. Linda and I read it together:

```
Mrs. Clark. Stop.
Trip more profitable than expected. Stop.
Will extend trip by at least 6 mos. Stop.
Keep watch on house. Stop.
```

Fortunately, Silas had intercepted it, but he made a beeline over to interrogate us. For the moment at least, he seemed to be willing to keep the news from Mrs. C, but he would need satisfactory answers from us.

"So it looks like the McGrews are going to be late in returning?" I started cautiously, not knowing where to go next or where Silas' mind had already taken all of us. "I guess that's good news for us, huh? It gives us more time to find a house of our own and we can be neighbors that much longer."

"Yes, we really love having you and Mrs. C as neighbors," Linda added.

Silas hesitated and then asked, "Joe, what's your deal? Are you grifters? Did you just come here looking for some free room? I don't get it! I mean you have a very nice family and well to tell the truth, I can't think of a thing either of you have ever done or said to make me not trust you. But it just doesn't add up. And the things Sammy says that make no sense…"

"Silas," I interjected, "she's a five year old! They don't always *make* sense!"

"Things like what?" Linda asked.

"Well like the other day, when I was reading her one of her books and she said she was tired and wanted to go upstairs and watch TV. Who the hell is *TV*?"

"That's what you're upset about, Silas?" Linda asked as she leaned toward him and grasped his hand.

Silas pulled his hand back slowly as his expression hardened. Looking straight at us, he asked, "What are their names?"

"Whose names?"

"The members of the McGrew family?" he shot back.

"You mean Cousin Mary and her husband Angus? Linda answered without hesitation.

"Go on," Silas insisted. "Name their kids."

"Oh, I don't believe this, Silas!" Linda spat back as she burst into tears (another of her specialties).

"How about you? Can you tell me the names of the kids?" he asked turning on me.

I looked to Linda for some sign or hint, but she had turned her back on both of us and turned up the volume. "I have no idea. They're Linda's cousins! I've never met them! What's this all about, Silas?" I insisted as I offered some very insincere comfort to Linda's shoulder.

Silas turned and looked downward. More silence and then a long breath from Silas. Linda had apparently run out of fake tears. Finally, Silas spoke. "Here's what I know. I think the world of the two of you and your family. It has been a pleasure to know all of you. But something is wrong with your story, and that makes me feel uneasy, that's all. In McGrew's telegram, why didn't he make any mention of you two living in his house? When he left, he asked me to keep an eye on it, so I would think he'd have mentioned it."

His eyes swept both of ours and he rose to leave. This time I reached out to him. "Silas, we think the

86

world of you too, as well as Mrs. C. You're right; there is something wrong. We are facing some problems. We had no choice about coming here to Marshalltown to live, and we also had no place to turn. When Linda realized that her cousin was gone to Europe we just moved in; they know nothing about us living here. We just know if they did, they would open up their house to us."

"And they would know we would treat it just like it was our own," Linda sniffled.

Silas looked directly at us again, but now the accusatory fire was out, only the kindness of his brown eyes showed. "Is there anything I can do?" he asked.

"You've already been a tremendous help to us, Silas!" I answered. "But we have to solve this ourselves."

"OK," he said, "I understand. But all you have to do is ask, you know." Turning back, he reached for Linda's hand and pulled her to him for a big hug. "I'm sorry I upset you Linda. I didn't want to, but I had to ask. The telegram just raised so many questions. You'll let me or Mrs. Clark know if there is anything we can do to help?" Linda nodded, still wiping fake tears.

"Just one thing, Silas. Let us break the news to Angus and Mary. We can send them another telegram."

"Alright," he promised as he headed out the door. "We'll leave it up to you." He waved, and then stopped as if he had just remembered something. Turning around to us again, he suddenly asked, "Where did you ever find that book Sammy had?"

"Which one was it?" Linda inquired cautiously.

"It was new looking, had lots of very pretty colored pictures of the little horse," Silas offered.

"Oh, *My Little Pony*," Linda guessed, turning to look out the window to avoid making eye contact. "We, um, brought that with us."

"Really a cute story for a little girl," Silas observed, "but the copyright date in the book was 19*99*, not 19*09*. A misprint, I suppose. Anyway, I knew she didn't find it here in the McGrews' house; they don't have *children*. But then, you already know that." And, with that, he turned and left. We were both sure we saw a wink in his eye as he turned.

Linda and I just looked at each other for a long time. Finally I broke the silence. "Can you believe this? Now what do we do?"

"I don't know, Joe, but we're going to have to do something and soon because I don't know what he's going to tell her, but if I know Mrs. C., she isn't going to be satisfied until she gets *something* out of him. She'll keep asking questions until she has us painted in a corner so badly we'll have no choice. I think it will go a lot better if we can keep feeding him a little of the truth at a time and let him get used to it slowly."

"So do I," I agreed. "*If* they give us that much time."

Nate and Abby came in from playing stickball with Georgie; we could see Georgie hanging around the front step. "Mom," Nate started, "we think you need to talk to Georgie."

"Well, we all have a pretty big mess to deal with right now thanks to Silas," Linda answered.

"Yeah, what's with him? We tried to talk to him, but he just walked on by us like he didn't see us coming at the corner!"

"He's getting very suspicious about us and why we're here."

"Well *somebody* needs to talk to Georgie—now!" Nate insisted. "Mom, Dad, he needs help!"

Linda and I glanced at each other and then rushed to the window. In addition to the usual layers of dirt, Georgie was also sporting various bruises and crusted abrasions and a very healthy shiner. However, as he turned and faced the street to look at a passing carriage we saw a fresh blood stain on the seat of his pants.

"Did you kids have a fight?" I asked stupidly, but all I got for my efforts was stunned silence and looks that told me how incredibly dumb they thought I was.

Linda took charge immediately. "Abby, take Sammy up to her room and read to her. And shut the door! Nate, go get me some bandages and the peroxide." For once, they both complied without a bit of chin music. "And you," she barked in my direction. "Oh, never mind, just wet a washcloth and come out on the porch with me. I was afraid of this."

Georgie's condition didn't improve one bit under closer scrutiny. Someone had beaten the kid severely—and worse apparently. As Linda tried in vain to dab some of the thickest of the blood and dirt off his wounds, she looked up at me with a combination of anger and fear that I had never seen in her before. "I'll get Silas," I whispered. I bounded from our front porch to his in three giant steps and entered the front door without knocking, setting back my standing with Mrs. C at least a dozen notches. "Mrs. C, we need Silas immediately and tell him to bring his bag," I yelled as if he would go anywhere without it.

"Dr. Fischer, come quickly. It's the Murphys!" she yelled down the hall. Turning to me, she asked quickly, "Is it one of the children?" I just nodded and turned back toward our porch.

Silas was surprised to see that the patient wasn't one of our kids, but he sized the situation up quickly and ushered Georgie back to his office. He instructed Mrs. C to run a warm bath and to find several clean towels. Then to our extreme surprise, he asked if Linda would mind assisting him in examining Georgie. Without hesitation, she agreed and directed me to go back and be with the kids. She was gone for over an hour; when she returned she looked exhausted. She didn't have much to say other than that she would like to know how anyone could do that to a child. Silas was going to keep him overnight and had asked Mrs. C to buy him some new clothes in the morning.

"So his dad did this?" I asked. She nodded. "Shouldn't we call the Department of Welfare? Or the police?"

"Silas said he would take care of it! Joe, he can't *ever* go back to live with that man. Mrs. C is trying to find a family for him to stay with until something permanent can be found."

We didn't talk about it again that evening; mainly we just acted as if everything would be all right while we each processed the horror of it. Some things have not changed even since 1909. I knew that Linda wanted to take him in, and I wondered why she didn't just come out and say so. Perhaps she was being practical, or maybe she had reasoned that we dared not keep him in our house for fear that when "it" happened, he might wind up in 2009 along with us. I couldn't be sure, but

I felt certain we weren't finished with this matter. My last thought that night was that I would check with Silas first thing in the morning to make sure he sicked the authorities onto Georgie's father.

I woke during the night and found that I was alone in bed. I felt Linda's side of the sheet; it was still warm. She returned and re-occupied the real estate on her side of the bed. Reading my mind, she said, "I'm fine, I just needed a drink. Go back to sleep."

Easy enough orders to carry out; I complied within minutes. When the sun woke me in the morning, Linda was still sawing logs, so I closed the door and let her sleep. I made breakfast for the kids and played with Sammy until Linda rolled out at 9:30. She did not look rested, but I assumed Georgie's ordeal continued to torment her. As soon as she looked steady enough to man the fort, I went next door to check with Silas. He assured me that he had made a call to "the authorities" and that they would investigate the situation. He said they would take the necessary steps to ensure Georgie's continued safety. I couldn't ask for more than that.

Satisfied that Silas had handled the situation, I moved on to the matter of his curiosity about our origins. "Silas, are we OK on the issue from yesterday? I mean as far as where we came from, why we're here, and so on?"

He looked at me with the kind side of those brown eyes and said, "Joe, yesterday I acted out of concern. I thought I had to get down to the truth in order to protect the McGrews' property as I promised. I was afraid you two were up to something harmful or maybe illegal. I let my suspicions overrule my gut feeling that you and

Linda are both honest, respectable people who care about your kids, all kids. I'm no longer concerned about the McGrews' house." He paused for a bit, "But I'm still concerned. I know you two are dealing with something that makes for heavy hearts. I don't know what it is, but I hope you'll tell me if you ever think it's my business. Just know that I would be happy to help in any way I can." Then, he added, "And so is Mrs. Clark in her own way."

"Silas, I really appreciate that you are willing to trust us!"

"I never said I trusted you; I just can't figure you out, that's all!" he laughed, as he slapped me on the back. "And besides, there's always been something odd about that house, so I'm not so sure it's all *your* fault."

I thanked him again for giving us the space to solve our own problems and for helping with Georgie and headed out the door. I reminded him that he still hadn't taken us up on our offer of dinner at Stones. I was congratulating myself on such fine work as I entered our house, dying to tell Linda what I had learned, but the house sounded empty. Then Sammy appeared at the head of the stairs and greeted me with "Daddy!" as she raced down the steps. "Where is everybody, Sammykins?" I asked as I scooped her up.

"Nate and Abby went to find Georgie."

"Where's Mommy?" I asked a little worried.

"Up in her bed," she answered matter-of-factly.

I climbed the steps two at a time and found Linda in bed just as Sammy said. I stroked her hair and woke her. "Are you sick, hon?"

"I don't know. I'm just so tired."

"Well, you had a big ordeal yesterday." I assured her not believing my own words. "Have you had any coffee yet?"

"Yes, but it didn't help. I just don't have any energy."

"Maybe you have a bug or something. Maybe it's mono, you know the *kissing disease*!" I added as I planted a big wet one on her lips. Sammy and I were at least twice as amused as Linda was over that one. "Come on downstairs and have some oatmeal and juice with us. That'll perk you right up!" I pulled her up into a sitting position against her will and tried to get her to put one foot ahead of the other one, but I was slugged on the arm for my efforts.

"Leave me alone. I'll come down when I'm ready!" With that, she headed for the bathroom and I took Sammy downstairs for what was probably her second breakfast.

We never made it to the kitchen. Nate and Abby burst in the front door with a very different-looking Georgie. He sported new clothes and the dirt was all but gone, but so was his enthusiastic attitude. He now seemed sullen and angry. "I *hate* you!" he shot at me as soon as he laid eyes on me.

"Georgie! What's the matter?"

"What's the matter is now I has to live with that ol' lady Watters and all her *foster* keeds! I used to have me own room and things was mine. Now I gotta sleep wit four *other* boys. What the hell good's that?"

"I see," I said, trying to comfort him. "But hey, how about those new clothes? Don't you like having new, *clean* clothes?"

He just scowled at me.

"He wants to go back to his dad!" Abby explained.

Armed with this information, I tried to help Georgie make sense of his situation, all the while wondering what the social workers had told him or how he would fare in front of the judge when that day came. "Son, I know things are different for you now, but they couldn't let you go back to living where you got beaten and *hurt*, could they?"

"My dad just gets mean sometimes when he's drunk, but I know he won't do it again. He told me so!"

"When did he tell you that, Georgie?"

"Just before he passed out and I ran away. I gotta tell him where I am at least 'cause he'll be worried!"

"You know you can't go home and be with him, don't you? Not by yourself!" I reasoned.

"Already been home this morning, but he weren't there! Hasn't been there since the night I ran away!"

"How do you know that?"

"The neighbor told me some men came and argued with him the day I ran. They took him and he ain't been back since."

Something told me there was more to this story but that it would wait until Georgie had settled down a bit. "It's almost time for lunch, Georgie. Do you want to eat with us?"

I could see he gave it some serious consideration but in the end thought better of it. He finally said, "Naw, I gotta show up at ol' lady Watters' or I'll be in the shitter if I don't! It's one of her stupid rules."

"OK then, but Nate why don't you take Georgie home and then hurry back for your own lunch? Take the street car as far as you can, but make sure he *gets* to the Watters' house," I suggested. To my surprise, Nate's look told me he was on exactly the same page with me for a change.

As Nate and Georgie headed off, Abby and I started to make lunch. Sammy went upstairs to tell Linda we were cooking (probably to plead her case for something better). Eventually, Linda came down, still in her PJs; I could see she didn't feel like another interrogation, so I got her the glass of water she requested and let it pass.

"Dad, what's going to happen to Georgie?" Abby asked.

"I'm not sure, but I don't think he will be returning to live with his dad any time soon. Do you think he should be?"

"No, not after what his dad did, but well, it sounds like he still loves him, even after everything, you know, he's done to him," Abby replied. Abby's words summarized child abuse amazingly well.

"Yes, I think you're right. That's what makes dealing with abused children and their families so tough; there aren't any easy answers," I explained. "No matter how awful things are, the kids almost always want to return to their parents. I guess because it's what they know and are familiar with; what they have counted on. And they don't realize anything could be better."

Abby took a bite of her sandwich and mulled that over before observing, "Sort of like us wanting to get back to 2009?" Out of the mouths of babes. We all sat and chewed on that for a few minutes.

Then suddenly, changing the subject, Linda announced, "Joe, I think I *am* sick!"

CHAPTER 9

"Oh, hon, what's the matter? What is it, upset stomach, headache, what?"

"I've had both of those, but mainly I just don't have any energy. No matter how much I sleep, I just can't get going," she explained.

"Sounds like you're pregnant, Mom,"Abby diagnosed matter-of-factly. "I'd think you and Dad would know what to do by now," she added, clueless as to just how close to death she herself was coming.

"I'm NOT *pregnant*!" Linda assured.

"Well, you should let Silas have a look at you then. He's probably over there now. Go up and shower and dress and then let him check you out," I offered.

"Joe, he went to medical school 50, no, *150* years ago. *I* know more than *he* does! Besides, my symptoms indicate I have some sort of virus and even in 2009 there wouldn't be anything they could do about that."

She had a point, but she had always told me anyone who tries to treat himself has a fool for a patient. And, no matter what she felt about Silas' credentials, he would be an objective set of eyes and ears she could at least consult with. Besides, he had a rudimentary lab set up, so he should be able to perform a few basic tests. I knew we were both dreading the 1909 *treatment* as much the actual ailment, but slowly I convinced her. She promised that she would dress for the day and go see him as soon as she lay down and rested a bit. She asked that Nate, Abby, and I leave for a while so that she and Sammy could take naps and promised to see Silas later in the day. As Linda trudged up the stairs with Sammy, Nate returned from his mission to escort Georgie back to the Watters' house. I headed him off before he could blurt out his report.

We walked toward downtown, and Nate divulged what he had learned. As I feared, Georgie had been sneaking back to his shack whenever possible since the night he ran off and could not find any sign of his dad. And he was thinking of running away from the Watters' house as soon as his dad showed up.

Abby and I filled Nate in on Linda's health concerns. I reminded them of how much we depended on Linda for our future as a family; I did not dwell on the link between her survival and theirs! Our long walk also gave us another chance to discuss our 20th-century plight. We all had ideas; no one had solutions. Nate wondered if Linda's medical training and my skills as a counselor were the reason we were in 1909, maybe to meet

Georgie's needs somehow. Abby agreed with Nate. Frankly, it was as good an idea as anyone had come up with so far. Finally we decided that it surely couldn't hurt and since no one else seemed to be stepping up to help him, we probably should.

We turned south toward Linn Creek where Georgie's shack was located, to see if we could find any sign of his dad. Nate was able to lead us straight there. It was less than I had imagined, literally a tar paper shack built from lumber scraps, many of which had not even been cut to length, no larger than a single garage. No one was home and it looked like no one had been there since the night Georgie was last attacked. Bottles and broken dishes covered the floor and blood was obvious in more than one place; Georgie had apparently put up quite a fight. Abby turned away, sick, once she reconstructed the images in her mind.

From in front of the shack, I could see no sign of any neighbors other than one shack on the far side of the creek, which did have an unobstructed view of his house. I told the kids we should go to the bridge and cross over so I could find out what they knew. Abby wanted to stay and rest in the grass on the creek bank, so Nate and I headed for the neighbors' house.

We had just crossed the bridge when we heard Abby's sickening scream. She was standing on the edge of the creek, pointing up-stream under the bridge. I was certain what she had found, and I was right. A badly beaten man in his forties lay on the creek bank under the bridge. He was still alive, but it didn't look like that would be the case for long if he didn't get medical attention. Before I could even tell him, Nate took off on a dead run in the direction of our house; I knew he would be bringing Silas and more help. Ordering Abby to keep clear, I waded into the creek and up to the man under the bridge. One eye was swollen shut, but the other pleaded for help as it blinked away the blood and tears. I could tell from the familiar odor that this was indeed Georgie's dad. Judging from the blood in the crotch of his pants, he had endured more than a beating.

I dabbed at his head wounds with a wet hankie until I heard Silas and the police arrive. Then footsteps came over the bridge and two uniformed cops scurried down the bank with a stretcher.

As they carried him up out of the muck and into the daylight, I could make out a spot on the bank behind his shack where the grass and earth had been rearranged and spattered with blood (long ago dried) which was surely where he had been beaten and castrated. I noticed that neither of the police officers seemed the least bit sympathetic toward the man, and I assumed this wasn't their first call to his aid. As they hauled him off to the hospital in the police car, I pulled Silas aside. "What do you know about this?" I demanded.

"After treating that boy, I know he got *some* of what he had coming!" he answered almost coolly.

"Silas, did you have anything to do with this?" Before he could answer, I fired off the second accusation. "I'm no doctor, but it looks to me like that man has been castrated! I thought you were going to turn Georgie's matter over to the authorities?"

"I did damn it!" Silas fired back. "Who the hell do you think 'the *authorities*' are?" As he turned to go, he added, "And I think they handled it very appropriately too. Oh, he'll live, might even make it to old age. But I'm pretty sure he won't be bothering that boy again!" Once behind the wheel, he asked, "Are you and Abby coming or not?"

Before I could answer, Abby said "No thank you! We'll walk!" Waving as if to say "suit yourself," Silas drove off in his T in the direction of Main Street. Abby put her arm around my waist and hugged me before she burst into tears. I tried to explain why anyone would have done that to Georgie's dad and offered what assurances I could come up with that we would not have to live in 1909 forever. Once she quit crying, we headed home. I knew she was very confused by what she had seen and heard. We both were. One thing was sure; I had put way too much faith in "the system," such as it was, in 1909. Modern-day authorities would never have done this to Georgie's dad. What was less obvious was which system I believed in more at that time.

By the time we reached our house, Linda was up and dressed and talking to Nate. He had of course told her about the entire ordeal, complete with every detail. "Dad, will Georgie's dad be all right? I mean, will he live?" Nate demanded as soon as we entered the house.

"According to Silas, he will," I assured him, only somewhat convinced myself. "How are you feeling hon?" I asked Linda as I felt her forehead.

"Much better, thank you," she answered managing a smile. "That nap with Sammy worked wonders. I guess I just haven't been getting enough sleep. Joe, what's going to happen to Georgie?"

"Well, for one thing, I don't think he'll be getting any more mistreatment from his father. And, I suppose after the old man heals up enough, Georgie will go back to living with him. I really don't know what else we can do for him, except keep checking on him day to day.

"For now, I think we have enough to do to take care of our own family to get you well! Let's get you over to the good Dr. Silas' place for an exam and find out what the problem is!" I added.

"Not today! I feel fine now. If I get to feeling bad again, I will go see him, but there's no use when the symptoms have gone away. He'd have enough trouble diagnosing the problem when I'm truly sick."

She sounded like the Queen of Denial, and yet she made sense on some level, so I agreed in silence.

CHAPTER 10

Aside from winter, Iowa only has one other "season'" August, and in 1909 it brought even more heat. Sleep was hard to come by until after midnight most nights, and opening the windows only let the humidity pour in like floodwaters. The sleepless nights did afford Linda and me many opportunities to hash and rehash our situation; no amount of scrutiny, however, resulted in any solutions. As far as we could tell, we were going to live out the rest of our days in the first part of the 20th-century.

By the middle of August, Linda and I started thinking about the approaching school year, as if we actually had any say in the matter. We certainly weren't looking forward to putting our children into 1909 schools (in Marshalltown or anywhere else), and yet neither of us could state any valid reasons for our hesitation except that a 20th-century education wouldn't serve our kids very well if somehow we ever made our way back to the 21st-century. Or would it?

We were even more concerned about the growing attachments our kids were making to 1909 friends. That ship had pretty much sailed in the case of Georgie, of course, but 1909 members of the opposite sex were looking better and better to Nate and Abby. We had cautioned both of them repeatedly about getting involved with significant others, but we were seeing few signs our cautions were being heeded. The start of school would only fuel those fires. Of course, it was far too late to prevent Sammy from forming an attachment to Silas; she clung to him like a barnacle every chance she got.

No, those long sleepless nights gave us far too much time to think. Inevitably, our discussions came back to Silas and Mrs. C and how and when to reveal the facts of our situation to either of them. We were certain that Silas suspected there was more to our situation than we had admitted but that he was OK with that. Mrs. C was another matter altogether. Her loyalty and devotion to Silas made her suspicious in ways that would put Homeland Security to shame.

That was our predicament. In order to keep Mrs. C off our backs, we were going to have to keep giving Silas larger and larger bits of the truth. We felt he would be OK with just about anything we revealed to him and was more than capable of using it to keep Mrs. C in check. We could not trust even Silas to act wisely if privy to too much information about the future. We knew we had to be extremely cautious in feeding our facts to him.

We thought the safest avenue into a discussion of the fact that we had already lived through the later half of the 20th century was through Silas' interest in sports. Nate's collection of sports trivia books afforded Linda and me the necessary edge to broach our previous history through a show of clairvoyance in any sport. When Linda discovered that the first race event ever at Indianapolis Speedway had taken place on August 12, 1909, she tried to start a discussion about racing with Silas, but he acted as if she had taken leave of her marbles. Clearly, he was not destined to become a NASCAR fan. Our further attempts to discuss sports with Silas soon proved that baseball was his only sports interest.

We lucked out completely later in August when his beloved Pittsburgh Pirates moved into first place in the National League with an impressive win average of 0.723, far ahead of Chicago's 0.670. By the first day of school, on September 7, only Chicago, Cincinnati, and the New York Giants were any threat. The race was down to the Cubs and the Pirates by the third week in September, and the Pirates clinched the title by the first week in October, assuring that they would be in the 1909 World Series.

Initially we played with Silas a bit, encouraging him to place small bets for a quarter or a beer with his buddies on Main Street, steering him in the direction of the team destined to win, but as the time for the series neared, we could see we had created a monster. With the fervor typical of a hard-core baseball fanatic, he started raising both the brag factor and the wager size with each win of the remaining regular season. By the morning of October 9, when Silas read the headline that the Pirates had won the first game of 1909 World Series 4 to 1 against the Detroit Tigers, he felt unstoppable. Never pausing to question our uncanny knack for predicting the outcomes of the games, he began a downhill slide into a place from which we began to fear he could not return.

Silas refused to believe our prediction that the Tigers would be victorious in game 2 and bet a total of $28 dollars with his cronies, but being both a man of honor and a die hard Pirate, he immediately placed the same bets on the Pirates with the same cronies for game 3 on October 11. With those winnings he flew right back into the flames of defeat when the Tigers won game 4, 5-0.

Before game 5 on October 13, the series was divided 2-2. Linda and I sat Silas down on our porch and tried to get him to lay off the betting, but we could tell by the glazed-over look in his eyes we'd stood a better chance trying to reason with Sherman on the outskirts of Atlanta. His Main Street buddies were razzing him unmercifully and we could not dissuade him. The only thing he wanted from us was our "prediction" about the outcome so he would know how heavily to bet. Wanting no part of his further demise, we held off giving him any predictions at all (knowing the Pirates would prevail and that he would never bet against them). For those actually in attendance, the game probably looked like a runaway for the Pirates with their 3-1 lead until the top of the 6th inning, when Ty Cobb scored on Sam Crawford's double and Crawford made it in before the end of the inning, tying up the game.

Moreover, in the bottom of the 6th, the Pirates added nothing to the scoreboard but another zero. Then they held the Tigers at 3 in the seventh and scored four runs themselves in the seventh and one more in the eighth for a final score of 8-4.

The seesaw that was the 1909 World Series had just tilted back to the Pirates side of the ledger and the next day Silas was almost uncontainable. While the actual game was underway, we pinned him down for another discussion about the importance of balance and reason, but with absolutely no effect; after all, we were talking about sports, baseball in particular, and we were talking to one of the most headstrong, stubborn men in town. Finally, Linda blurted out, "Silas, they lose game six, 4 to 5! Everyone thinks this will be the last game; there will be the poorest attendance of the Series, but they lose and have to play the seventh game!"

The silence was deafening. The only sounds we heard outside the window early on the morning of October 14 were the robins as we all drew very cautious breaths.

"What do you mean, they *lose*? How could you possibly be so sure of that?" Silas demanded.

"I'm so sure of it Silas, I will bet you $25 and if the final score isn't 4-5 for the Tigers, I'll pay you $50," Linda snapped back, looking at me not so much for approval as for some sign of support. Since the typical teacher in 1909 made only $40 per month, Linda was talking a major chunk of change.

There was another long silence from Silas, but had he voiced his thoughts he would have needed a megaphone. His brow furrowed deeply as he mulled over Linda's challenge, rolling his lucky silver dollar in his hand. Suddenly he reached for his hat with one hand

and his game five headlines with the other, rose with only a simple "Well, good day then," and headed for our front door.

"What about the bet, Silas?" Linda continued after him.

"Linda, leave him alone!" I chided.

Whirling around, Silas offered only that he didn't take winnings from a *lady* and again excused himself. The look on his face left no doubt that he was disappointed and maybe a bit angered by Linda's challenge, but one thing was clear—once he read the headline about game six and learned the outcome of the game, he would be back for more information. Linda had baited the hook and set it. Now we had to figure out whether to keep him or throw him back once we reeled him in.

Nate kept an eye on Silas' front porch on the morning of the 15th. As soon as he saw the paperboy coming up the walk, he yelled to us, but Silas was already out the door and bent over the paper, plucking it off his porch floor. He glanced at the headline, glared in our direction, and then plopped down on his front step. Shaking his white head, he skimmed through the paper for the box scores as if searching some hint as to how the hell Linda had nailed the outcome so accurately or an explanation of how his beloved Pirates could have let him down.

We realized we had to play our next move *very* carefully. If we didn't make our prediction specific enough to be convincing, we might miss our best chance; if we overwhelmed Silas with too many facts about the final game, we'd alienate him, perhaps permanently. No, we had to find exactly the right piece of trivia that would convince Silas that we in fact had detailed advance knowledge of the game without crushing his ego or giving away the outcome. Nate found just the ticket in a footnote in his sports encyclopedia.

All day on the 15th, we watched for some sign that Silas was still speaking to us, but he had not emerged from his house even once by late afternoon. Finally, Linda consulted with Mrs. C, who confessed her concerns about Silas. She was used to seeing him make a fool of himself over baseball, but he usually only talked it up with his friends, seldom betting more than beer money. In fairness, he'd not had any reason to get too excited because his Pirates' only other series appearance in 1903 against the Boston Americans (which they had lost five games to three). But this time was very different. Not only had he taken to bragging and boasting to his friends, but also Mrs. C suspected that he'd made wagers for much more than beer money. Since the Pirates' loss in the sixth game, he'd stayed in his office, not even coming out for lunch. He just sat in there puffing on one cigar after the next rereading the same newspaper article about the game and shooing away all but the most critical of patients. Sensing the extent of Mrs. C's worries, we were careful not to fan the fires, but offered to speak to him for her.

"Silas, Joe and Linda are here to see you," Mrs. C started.

"Tell them to go away and not come back 'til after the game!" was his reply.

At that, Mrs. C stepped briskly into his office, closing the door tightly behind her, and made a beeline for the back of Silas' chair. We could hear only muffled tones, but a deaf man sitting behind a pole could have guessed that Silas was getting the benefit of Mrs. C's opinion, and the vast majority of what was said was said by Mrs. C. Every time he tried to speak, Mrs. C cut him off and each attempt grew briefer. Finally, we heard the unmistakable squeaks of his desk chair as he rose and trudged toward the door. With his cane in one hand and his wadded up newspaper in the other, he emerged from his office. "Well, what is it? Have you come over to . . . " Silas halted abruptly after catching Mrs. C's eye.

More silence. Reaching for his hand, and looking into his eyes, Linda made the first move. "Silas, I wanted to apologize to you if I in any way diminished your enjoyment of the game."

More silence as Silas looked down at the floor as if searching for a contact. "Accepted! It's forgotten about!" With that, he looked up and asked, "so is it going to rain?"

Judging from the smoke billowing from the open door way to his office, I guessed that Silas' other great weakness, food, might be the way to get him over to our house. "Silas, Linda made an apple pie today. Why don't you join us for supper?" Never accused by anyone of being slow on the uptake, Mrs. C explained that she had had a very trying day and wanted to take it easy in her room the rest of the evening. "You go enjoy yourself with the Murphys, Dr. Fischer. You've been under a lot of pressure lately," she directed as she patted him on the wrist and headed down the hall toward her quarters. This was a major improvement over the "Listen, you stubborn old coot" speech we had imagined we missed moments earlier.

No one said much on the way over to our house; the little conversation we had was not about baseball. Linda made a real feast of fried chicken, mashed potatoes, and green peas, and, of course, she did have an apple pie. Sammy sat next to Silas and did her best cute little girl number for Silas. Nate and Abby even joined us for supper and managed to steer the after-dinner conversation to the topic of baseball. We eventually talked about the wondrous season the Pirates had had. The glow returned to Silas' cheeks as he related just how smoked his friends down on Main Street had been about the Pirates edging the Cubs out. Yes, things were getting back to normal and we were well on our way to being back in Silas' good graces.

We cleared the table and put Nate and Abby to work washing and drying the dishes while Linda, Silas, and I moved to the parlor. Because it was Linda who had offended Silas, she led off with another apology. Silas cut her short by reminding her that he'd agreed to forget all about it. "Silas, I need to have you hear me out. Please?" Linda began again. "I am truly sorry if I spoiled the game for you. I know how much you love the Pirates and baseball, and well, we do too. However, you have to let us explain something. Something more important than baseball." She had his attention.

"There is a very good reason why I was able to tell you what would happen in game six. In fact, I could tell you everything that will happen in the final game. So could Joe or Nate or Abby. But don't worry we're not going to."

Silas looked as if he was about to bolt, but since his cane was in the umbrella stand in the hall, he'd have a devil of a time getting up off the couch without help. Linda assured him again that we weren't going to spoil the game for him in any way. He gave her a look like a beaten pup and asked, "Why are you doing this?"

"Silas," I began, "we've been trying to find a way to explain something to you, something extremely important, but which will be very hard for you to believe. We just wanted a way to make it easier for you to accept."

I might as well have been speaking in Chinese.

"Joe, what in God's name are you talking about? I've already figured out that you somehow got word of the game by telegraph from Detroit, probably by sending Nate to the Western Union." We both laughed out loud and *that* did *not* help our case.

"Silas, I told you the final score *while* the game was *still being played!*" Linda reasoned.

"That was just pure luck. Wasn't it?" Silas asked, giving the first hint that we were getting to him.

"No, Silas, it wasn't!" Linda paused. "I don't know enough about baseball or the Pirates to make predictions with any accuracy. I was able to tell you the score because I read it in a book. A book that was published in…" Linda stalled as she pulled Nate's Encyclopedia of Baseball off the shelf across the room and thumbed through the first few pages. "…in 1999!"

"That's preposterous!" Silas exploded. "How could that be? That's 90 years from now!"

"See for your self, Silas," Linda urged gently, her tone softening as she sat next to him.

"Just because it says it here doesn't make it so. You could have had it printed to say that. And that still doesn't prove you didn't try to cheat me!"

"OH!" Linda exclaimed as she yanked the book out of Silas' hands and paced across the parlor. Our heated discussion had brought Abby in from the kitchen, followed by Nate drying the last plate.

"It's true what she's telling you, Silas," Abby assured. "That book was published in 1999 and we have many others like it upstairs. We have hundreds of things in our house that you couldn't find any where else, because…"

"What do you mean 'your house'? This house belongs to the McGrew family!" Silas erupted.

"What Abby means," Linda interrupted, "is that we have many things here with us you've never seen yet. Because they are too new. And this is *our* house *now*. Or, at least it was *then*; Oh, crap! Joe, you explain it."

Before I could come up with anything close to intelligible, Nate took off his apron and stepped up to the plate, hitting one out of the park. "Silas, in the seventh game, Ty Cobb stands on first base, calls Honus Wagner a 'Kraut-head' and tells him he's going to steal second. Honus not only tags Cobb out, he tags him in the mouth and draws blood. You won't read this in the newspaper, but you will hear a rumor about it from your buddies after the game and for years to come."

CHAPTER 11

October 15, 1909- IOWA MONUMENT
LEVELED IN STORM THAT KILLS –
Shaft in Memory of Soldiers Who Fell
at Shiloh Destroyed in Severe Tornado

Silas sat silently for an eternity and then barked "Let me see that book!"

"No, Silas!" Linda snapped. "Not until after the Series is over. We've done enough to spoil it for you."

Silas seemed somewhat satisfied with Linda's answer, if not our whole explanation. "So what are you telling me? That you're all clairvoyants? That you can all somehow tell the future? What do you do, read tea leaves? Or tarot cards?"

"No, just books," Abby answered.

I was aware that we were all slowly edging closer to Silas like zombies from some old movie. "Give him some space," I ordered. No one budged. "Silas, what we're telling you is that we're from another time. We know a lot about what will happen in the future because we are *from* the future. The year 2009 to be exact. We bought this house in 2006 when it was *98 years old*! We restored it to its original condition and filled it with antiques from the early 1900s. After we finished restoring it, we went to bed on June 5, 2009, and when we woke up the next morning, it was June 6, 1909! We're not from *any* other *place*, we're from another *time*! One hundred years from now! That's our 'story,' Silas!"

What followed was a pause so pregnant, I thought someone would have to induce labor! When Silas eventually reacted, he did so with his eyes. They darted around the room as if scanning for some sort of proof to the contrary. "That's a bunch of crap! There isn't anything in this room I haven't seen somewhere before!"

"OK, gang," I challenged, "show him what you've got!" Picking up the gauntlet, everyone scurried off to provide proof of life after 1909. For starters, Abby retrieved her cell phone from the desk and her driver's licenses (the real one *and* the fake one). Nate brought his MP3 player with music blaring through the ear bud, powered by what was left of the battery. Linda produced a plastic bowl from the kitchen. One by one we paraded marvels of the 21st century past Silas and demonstrated them to his utter amazement for the next 20 minutes. Sadly, as we surveyed the advances humankind had made in the last 100 years, they were a paltry lot. Nothing we could offer did any more than forestall a little boredom or keep the mold from growing on food for a few days longer. No solutions to war or poverty or racism or any of the other problems man had created. No more definitive answers to the question "Why are we here" other than "It's a mystery." All we could show him was two miniaturized noisemakers and a plastic lettuce-keeper (basically a Mason jar on steroids). I was afraid the irony of the situation did not escape Silas. We tried to explain the promise of computers and the Internet, but that one was hard enough to get across in the 21st century.

I think I expected Silas to be stunned into silence, but I badly underestimated the old goat. Instead of quiet resignation, he immediately had questions for us, lots of questions. Mostly, he tried to explore the chinks in our explanation. We, of course, had answers, but he also made honest attempts to see into the future. Would there be any more wars? When would they cure TB? Would that bastard, Taft, serve more than one term? (We actually had to look that one up, but our answer scored big points with Silas.)

Eventually, Silas turned to practical questions, some of the same ones we had. *How* and *why* did we get sent to 1909? What would it take to get us back to our own time? Moreover, the real conversation stopper: "Is it so bad here or is it just that much better in 2009?"

We listed all the crackpot ideas we had tried to reverse the situation and return to 2009. We also shared our theory that we had been catapulted back in time to correct some wrong, but we had to confess that we had no idea what that was. Silas listened quietly for the most part, speaking only to address what he perceived to be weaknesses in our story, each of which we explained to his satisfaction.

It was Linda whose testimony held Silas' interest the most. Once Silas thought to ask about medical advances, he was putty in her hands. Cancer wasn't quite the scourge in 1909 that it was in 2009, simply because most people died of something else before they had the chance to contract cancer. Still, it was definitely a death sentence in the early 20th century. Silas was amazed to learn that a cure still eluded researchers. He wasn't surprised to learn that modern medicine had concluded that lifestyle choices were mainly to blame for heart disease, but he refused to believe smoking was one of them or that smoking caused lung cancer. The concepts of the artificial heart, open-heart surgery, and the defibrillation device fascinated him.

He listed off more of the mundane diseases and conditions that he dealt with daily, either in his patients or personally. Was there a cure for gout? For the common cold? Arthritis? With the help of our ample collection of medical reference books, Linda answered each question to Silas' satisfaction. He marveled at the number of drugs available to relieve the pain of arthritis and was stunned when Linda described joint replacement and arthroscopic surgery. He was fascinated to learn that the management of diabetes was just over the horizon in 1922, when Banting would produce the first insulin from cows. Linda steered clear of the advances in family planning or the miracles of Viagra.

Eventually Linda called a halt to the medical seminar and suggested that we had kept Silas up way past his bedtime. He bellowed at the thought until he checked his pocket watch and saw it was 12:35 a.m. Linda promised to let him come back any time and look through our library. As we helped him up off the sofa, we had one more very serious discussion.

"Silas," I started, "you know you can't breathe a word of this to anyone, particularly not Mrs. C! Our lives won't be worth living if people in Marshalltown suspected any of this!"

"Oh and I suppose you think I'd get elected mayor if I was the one to try to spring this on Marshalltown? Hell no, I'm not discussing this with anybody! I'm not sure how much of it I even believe. And in the morning, I'll think it was all a dream." The twinkle in his eyes told us that as much as he didn't want to believe our explanations, he really *did*. We walked him toward the door, but he stopped and turned to look directly at both of us. His demeanor suddenly turned very serious. "So how much longer do you think you'll be here?" he asked.

"Silas, we have no idea. We're stuck here until somehow we're brought back the same mysterious way we got here in the first place," Linda answered.

Silas seemed relieved, if only briefly. "So is it so bad here? I mean now?"

"No," Linda answered obligingly.

"Was it so much better in 2009?"

"No," I answered to everyone's surprise. "It's not *about* bad or good. It's about what's *right*, where we fit in. This isn't *our* time; it's *your* time. If we spend the rest of our lives here, we'll never fit in. We'll be immigrants in our own town."

"You mean…"

"Yes, Silas, we're all from Marshalltown," Linda interrupted as she moved him toward the door. "Except for Joe. He's from Nebraska, but he's lived here most of his life." Silas seemed relieved to learn that we were natives, although he gave me a sour look for some reason. Nate offered to walk Silas home, but when they reached the door, Silas stopped at the threshold and looked out cautiously as if he expected a bucket of water to fall on him. He scanned up and down the streets, probably for proof that he was indeed stepping out into the morning of October 16, 1909. Turning back to us one last time, he pleaded, "If you could just tell me the score, I could really clean up with the boys!"

"Yes, we know! Good night, Silas!" Linda exclaimed as she gently pushed him out the door.

CHAPTER 12

October 16, 1909 – PITTSBURG
LEADS IN DECISIVE GAME

As soon as the newspaper landed on Silas' doorstep the following day, we heard his trademark bellow. We could hear him whooping it up through the walls of both houses as he told the good news to Mrs. C. As soon as the last patient left Silas' office that afternoon, he caught the first streetcar downtown and started rubbing it in to Tiger and Cub fans alike. His precious Pirates were the 1909 World Champions, having defeated the Tigers 8-0. Some time after 11 p.m. the police chief escorted him home and tucked him in bed, not so much because he was worried about Silas but because the chief was a Tigers fan, and had heard quite enough. It was clearly a day none of us would soon forget.

We worried that once in his cups, Silas might forget his pledge to us and start talking about our situation. However, he was either a man of his word or he realized that his friends wouldn't take kindly to finding out he'd had inside information during the World Series. We never detected any evidence (either from Mrs. C or anyone else in town) that he had breathed a word of our secret.

Having come clean with Silas and with the excitement of the World Series behind us, we had little else to be concerned with other than our children's reactions to school. Sammy was still too young to start school (although she had already learned her letters and numbers and could count to 50), but Nate and Abby had been attending classes at Marshalltown High School since the day after Labor Day and had very mixed feelings about it.

First of all, they both tired of taking their lunches and actually claimed to miss the lunches of their 2009 MHS cafeteria. They both complained that while the material in their classes was in many ways easier to master, their teachers seemed unbelievably picky insisting on neat penmanship, perfect spelling, and near perfect grammar. None of their teachers gave extra credit for class participation or attitude, which left Nate with very little choice but to actually study. Abby drew an afternoon of detention for guessing "World War II" as an answer on one of her history exams.

It was in the nonacademic areas where Nate and Abby both cleaned up. Both kids had plenty of natural sports ability (which Linda insisted came from *her* side of the family). They also had the advantage of many years of coaching in multiple sports as well as experience with superior equipment.

When Abby came home and announced that she had secured a spot on the girls' basketball team, we were stunned—not that she had made it, but by the fact that MHS *had* a girls team at all in 1909. We were also surprised when she took to the official girls' uniform: billowing bloomers tucked into long stockings and an oversized white smock with a huge neck scarf. The team looked more like pep club members than participants, but Abby proudly took her place with the other five girls on the court and did her best to adapt to the "old-fashioned" rules of girls' basketball.

Nate went out for football and fared amazingly well making the varsity team as a freshman. Though he was small, he was very fast and managed to carry the ball for two touchdowns during the season. They played all games during the day, because lighted fields were many, many years off. Nate held out hope of being able to play baseball, his favorite sport in the spring.

The fall passed quickly for us. I delivered lumber and Linda took care of Sammy and the house. We took turns going up to the high school for tongue-lashings about Abby's smart mouth and dress code violations and Nate's unwillingness to apply himself. The kids kept busy with school and sports. Linda and I attended their home games, at least when Linda was up to it. The duties of a stay-at-home Mom seemed to consume most of her time and energy.

By mid-November, we faced yet another crossroads in our life in 1909. The arrival of cold weather meant we all spent much more time indoors. We finally, after almost six months, *missed* TV. No one missed anything in particular. I missed the evening news, but it was nice to sit down to dinner without hearing about just how badly the government had screwed up the world that day. No, what we missed was the comfort of coasting through the weekends and evenings without having to create our own pastimes. We finally began to realize just how much we had depended on the mind-numbing time killer that was TV.

We all read and took turns reading to Sammy. We played board games. The kids listened to their music (until the batteries ran down) and Nate played his guitar quietly. Mostly we talked. Not so much anymore about getting back to 2009 or even *why* we had won the no-expense-paid trip back in time, but we just talked. We talked about the important things as well as the not-so-important.

Nate, we realized, had a very good grasp of the basics of education, though his grades had never shown it. He had demonstrated his ability to problem solve when we were still restoring the house, the few times we were able to get him to help us instead of playing baseball. During family discussions, he was coming up with amazing insights into the history of the time. During one mealtime discussion about President Taft, Nate pointed out that while Taft was a dedicated legal scholar who believed in the potential of law and arbitration to settle disputes, he ignored the dissension in his own party. According to Nate, this led to Taft being the only president in history to finish third in a race for re-election, behind Theodore Roosevelt and Woodrow Wilson in 1912. So impressed were we by his grasp of history that we pressed him about why he was carrying a D in that subject.

Abby, on the other hand, didn't show the slightest interest in the content of academic classes but honed her considerable talents of persuasion and charm into precision surgical instruments. She not only pulled better grades than in 2009, she did so largely by flattering her female teachers and flirting with the males. She was even getting on Mrs. C's good side.

After a particularly productive session with Mrs. C, Abby managed to con her into making turkey and trimmings for Silas and our entire family at Silas' house on Thanksgiving. Mrs. C didn't even know what hit her. As Abby delivered the invite to us later that day (attached to a loaf of freshly baked bread), Linda demanded to know what had prompted Mrs. C to be so benevolent. Abby assured her that all she did was "mention" to Mrs. C that on more than one prior holiday, our whole family had come down with food poisoning. As I was separating Linda's hands from Abby's throat, I reasoned with Linda that dining with Mrs. C and the good doctor would provide us with good company, pleasant conversation, and spare Linda a lot of work. And Abby would get a chance to show off her own culinary talents when I accepted the invitation and offered to have Abby make the pumpkin pie—from scratch! The thought of Abby being up to her elbows in pumpkin guts for a purpose other than making a jack-'o-lantern slowly painted a smile—a very broad-smile on Linda's lips.

So it was that on November 26, 1909, the Murphy family, dressed in their holiday best, trotted next door to Silas Fischer's house toting a relish plate and two pies, (Abby's pumpkin and Linda's cherry). Mrs. C graciously accepted our offerings and placed Abby's pie in

ROBERT KERR

the middle of the table and Linda's in the kitchen "for later."

Silas was in rare form, having already fumigated the house with his Havanas. He greeted me with a glass of brandy and invited Nate and me to sit by the fire in the parlor. Mrs. C whisked Linda, Abby, and Sammy off to the kitchen, not as much as participants or helpers but as student observers.

Silas' parlor was the very picture of 1909 comfort. In one corner, a mahogany Victrola played Scott Joplin tunes softly. The open-hearth fireplace with its marble surround graced the west wall of the room as its crackling flames toasted our front sides and sucked every last BTU of heat out of the house and up the chimney. Off to the right side of the fireplace stood an easel on which was displayed the front page of the October 16 newspaper with headlines declaring the Pirates as World *Series* Champions. I assumed the coronation of any team as "*World* Champions" would have to wait until at least one other nation started playing baseball.

Silas didn't mention the championship or baseball but it was clear that he wanted *us* to from the number of times his brown eyes darted to the easel and back to us as he uttered "Yes, sir; yes sir" to himself. Finally, Nate asked, "So Silas, did you hear what happened between Ty Cobb and Honus Wagner during the Series?" with a wry grin on his face. Silas responded first with a shower of sparks from his cigar and then a big grin followed by a roughing up of Nate's hair. "Yeah, I heard all right. All the guys were talking about it right after the Series." After a short reflective pause, Silas looked over his shoulder in the direction of the kitchen and continued in a low tone meant only for Nate's ears. "You know, if you'd told me what you knew earlier we could have really…," But Mrs. Clark's shrill call to come to the dining room interrupted him before he could finish.

There, at the head of the table, in front of Silas' chair, sat Mrs. Clark's golden brown turkey. Every holiday offering imaginable covered the remainder of the table infield: candied yams, dressing, potatoes and gravy, cranberries, freshly baked rolls with homemade apple butter, and, of course, Abby's pumpkin pie. As we were choosing our positions around the table, Linda slid her relish tray in between the dressing and the rolls, ignoring the stink eye she was getting from Mrs. C. Let the Thanksgiving merriment begin!

For the next hour, we passed the food, ate our fill, and got to know Mrs. C and Silas (particularly Mrs. C) much better. We swapped stories of past Thanksgivings, being careful to filter out any hints that all our recent turkey days had taken place in the next century. Noticing Sammy's squirms inside her freshly starched dress, Mrs. C asked Sammy what she *least* liked about Thanksgiving (a thinly veiled attempt to get more dirt on Linda's domestic skills). She boldly replied, "When Daddy yells those bad words during the football game."

"Oh, Sammy, he doesn't mean anything by that," Nate broke in. "That's just how we play the game, right, Dad?"

"Uh, sure. That's right! It's just part of the game! Where we come from, it's a tradition for the men to play football after Thanksgiving dinner and sometimes we get carried away and curse, which isn't Ok, but it happens, right, Linda?" Linda nodded in agreement as she wiped imaginary gravy from Sammy's face to keep her from issuing any additional bulletins about life in 2009.

Perhaps it was the turkey, or cranberries, or maybe she had even sampled a bit of Silas' brandy. Whatever the cause, something softened Mrs. C just a bit. During her report on Thanksgivings past, she talked for the first time about her earlier life. She described an idyllic life with Mr. Clark, who had had a promising career as a banker before he was lost to "consumption" (or tuberculosis, as we knew it). She looked wistfully at Sammy as she explained that she and Mr. Clark had not had children. And, she described the years since his death when she had worked for Silas as his housekeeper and nurse. She had little, if any, formal training, Silas having taught her everything she needed to know to assist him in his small practice.

When Linda began pressing Mrs. C for more details about her training, I changed the subject to Silas and his past. Having had enough brandy, Silas took up the segue. No amount of alcohol could have prepared us for what we were about to hear.

With a mixture of pride and melancholy in his voice, he told us that he had graduated from medical school in his early twenties. He married and settled in Butler, Pennsylvania, where he started a practice. His voice breaking slightly, he told about the birth of his daughter, Amy, just before he was taken away to serve as a surgeon in the Union Army. At that point, his demeanor began to change. He got up and helped himself to more brandy.

When he returned, he had an almost vacant look in his eyes. He sat silently for a few moments until Sammy begged, "Go on, Silas. Tell us about Amy!"

Looking up at her as if seeing her for the first time, Silas smiled slightly and replied simply, "Another time honey, another time." Staring across the table at the empty space between Mrs. Clark and Linda, he went on. "Anyway, there I was half a country away 'saving lives.' I couldn't save *theirs*!" He wiped tears from his eyes and took another sip of brandy. "And I saved damned few of the soldiers either. We did saw-bones butchery mostly. No supplies! No hospitals! Damn few nurses!"

"Silas, there are *children* present!" Mrs. C admonished. He went on without acknowledging her point.

"After Gettysburg, the futility got to me. It didn't matter what we did, the wounded died. Some before we got to them, the rest after." At that point, he looked up, made eye contact with all of us, and said, "I'll never forget it as long as I live. I've tried, but I can't!" as if swearing an oath.

"Silas," I offered, "that's what wars do. They change things. They change *people!* Not just the soldiers who fight, are wounded, or die. They change everyone!"

"You think I don't know that?" he barked at me. "What I can't *forget* is that I *gave up*! I took an *oath*, for Christ's sake!"

"Silas!" was warning number two from Mrs. C.

He apologized and took another sip of brandy. As if to close off the topic, he continued, "So after the war, I had no reason to return to Pennsylvania. I just followed the Iowa men from my unit up here. I took to the town and I liked the people, so I stayed on."

No one had any more questions for Silas (or Mrs. C), at least none that seemed appropriate at that time. After a brief lull, the conversation changed to the upcoming Christmas season, caroling, trees, and, of course, Santa. I could see the wheels turning in Linda's head as the conversation unfolded. I assumed she was dreaming of Christmas shopping in the Victorian era, but she surprised me. With a wry look on her face, she thanked Mrs. C and Silas for the delicious dinner and their company and proposed that they let us repay them by spending Christmas Day at our house. Silas readily accepted, although Mrs. C reminded him that it wouldn't be right to intrude on our family on such a special day.

"Nonsense, woman! If they didn't want us, they wouldn't have invited us, right, Linda?"

Linda affirmed, "Absolutely! We'd be honored to have you, and I'd be honored to prepare Christmas dinner for you both!" Then, in a pristine example of where Abby had come by her powers of manipulation, Linda suggested we all have some of Abby's pumpkin pie. She carefully cut it into *six* pieces before passing it around the table. By the time the pie plate made it around to Mrs. C, it was empty. Linda then offered her sympathies at Mrs. C's missing out on the dessert derby and excused herself, returning promptly with a large piece of her cherry pie, just for Mrs. Clark. War *can* be hell!

CHAPTER 13

According to the calendar, winter officially starts on the 21st day of December, but in Iowa, it can start anytime after Labor Day. During the first week of December, Marshalltown received a snowfall that would have made the average person start humming, "Here Comes Santa Claus" and reach for the nearest copy of It's A Wonderful Life if either had existed then. Instead, the merchants of Marshalltown did what their modern-day counterparts do; they staged their store windows to separate their customers from as much cash as possible before the final bell on the 25th. Main Street storefronts began to resemble the illustrations in "The Night Before Christmas." Simple pine boughs and red ribbons decorated the streetlights. Brightly colored glass ornaments sparkled in store windows. What the merchants offered was delightfully simple. No displays of cheaply made, imported junk. No blaring electronic holiday music. No shelves of "gift items" whose only purpose in life was to collect dust. Only high-quality, handmade clothing and textiles graced the display cases of the clothing stores. Hardware store windows featured goods decked in holiday trimming and showcased bikes, wagons, and various other examples of items that appealed to kids.

Armed with the proceeds of the sale of another of my Eclipse Mining and Milling stock certificates, Linda took aim at an unforgettable old-time Christmas. Over the weeks between Thanksgiving and Christmas, she took every member of the family Christmas shopping at least twice. She hauled home winter clothing for all of us by the armload. Carried away by the experience of celebrating an old-fashioned Christmas, I went temporarily insane, shopping for jewelry for Linda. Nate and Abby were well past the Santa stage of their lives, but for some reason, they took to stockpiling gifts for their little sister like never before. They even picked out a baseball glove just the right size for Georgie. We all kept our eyes open for just the right gifts for Silas and Mrs. C.

By December 20, Sammy, with the help of Nate and Abby, had begged and pleaded more than enough, and we decided it was time to locate a Christmas tree. I was able to borrow the team and a sleigh from Fred and took the whole family, even Sammy, out east of town, where we spent the afternoon locating the perfect tree. Abby and Nate were actually civil to one another and saw that Sammy had great fun making snow angels and a snowman. It had been a long time since we had had such fun as a family. By dinnertime that evening, our parlor sported a freshly cut spruce tree on a homemade stand courtesy of Nate and me. The kids were stunned when I told them we would have to forgo the use of electric lights, but their complaints went away once Linda had them stringing popcorn and cranberries for the tree.

I really think the whole family was more excited about Christmas than they had been in years. Abby helped Sammy compose her letter to Santa and passed it to me to "mail." Without a constant barrage of TV ads telling her what she should want, Sammy had no choice but to form her Santa wish list from the items she saw in the store windows. This made shopping for her a breeze. By the time Christmas Eve came around, we were all about to burst, particularly Sammy.

We opened our gifts from each other on Christmas Eve; Santa, of course, brought his contributions during the night. It was actually heart-warming to see Abby so excited about such simple gifts as clothing, a diary, and hair ribbons. Nate absolutely drooled over the guitar we found at E. A. Tuffree Music. My buckskin mittens with wool liners would come in very handy as I delivered lumber in the cold months ahead. Linda said I looked "hot" in the fur hat from Nate and Abby, her little joke with the kids. Top honors went to yours truly, when Linda opened the hand-carved cameo locket with room for pictures of all three kids inside. She put it on Christmas Eve and never took it off again. For the first time ever, though, Linda and I felt that the kids were actually more interested in each other's company as a family than in amassing a pile of Christmas booty. It was likely the best Christmas any of us had ever experienced.

With Christmas Day still ahead, we expected the joy to continue. Silas rang the doorbell promptly at 11 a.m., leading an unwilling Mrs. C. Though we had no proof, we were certain she had "pre-eaten" just to be on the safe side. She arrived, toting cranberry sauce and candied yams, not wanting to chance what Linda might do to her two favorite Christmas treats.

Silas was in such good spirits, all he needed to complete his impersonation of the jolly old elf was a red suit. He carried a basket of gifts and a bottle of brandy; he slid the gifts under the tree but he retained full control of the brandy.

However, our guest of honor was Georgie. Nate and Abby had talked Mrs. Watters into letting him spend the afternoon with our family. While it certainly wasn't his first Christmas, it may have been the first one celebrated with good food or gifts and was undoubtedly the first one without fear. A barely recognizable Georgie showed up promptly at 11 carrying a jar of Mrs. Watters' homemade strawberry preserves with a big green bow on the side.

"Here, these is for you, 'cause it's Christmas!" he told Linda as he made his way into the house. Abby had no trouble convincing him he'd be much more comfortable without his mud and snow-caked shoes. Georgie sported new wool knee pants, stockings, and handknitted wool sweater about which he appeared torn. On one hand, he was extremely proud of it; on the other hand, he found the wool extremely uncomfortable. To top it all off, he had been scrubbed within an inch of his life and bore no olfactory resemblance to his former self. Once inside, he joined Sammy in "guarding" the presents under the tree lest one or more of them disappear.

Ordinarily, we would have saved the opening of presents until after dinner, but Sammy and Georgie simply could not wait and Silas was nearly as bad. Ever flexible, Linda and Abby made the necessary adjustments to the dinner timetable and we proceeded with the organized carnage that is a Christmas gift exchange. Nate and Abby abdicated their roles as Santa and directed Georgie in passing out the gifts. Since Santa had already visited our house the night before, our Christmas Day loot pile was down to a tasteful size.

Silas and Mrs. C went together on gifts for each of the children. Sammy loved her M. A. Donohue <u>History of Tom Thumb</u> storybook. Georgie was thrilled with the baseball from Nate, but he beamed with pride when he opened their gift of a shiny pocketknife. I thought he was going to faint when he opened the ball glove from our family. Nate showed him how to form a pocket in his glove and took him outside to play some catch when the pleading became unbearable.

Linda received some very nice handmade handkerchiefs and a collection of Mrs. C's favorite recipes handprinted in a finely bound book. I was the recipient of a copy of <u>The Trail of the Lonesome Pine</u> by John Fox Jr. and a beautiful handmade wool neck scarf.

As appreciative as we were of our presents, our gifts to Silas and Mrs. C left them speechless. Linda had found a genuine cameo pin for Mrs. C and a silver money clip for Silas. As a family, we had decided to give each of them a framed photo of the five Murphys. Silas actually had to excuse himself while he stepped in the dining room to wipe away tears when he opened his picture. He gave Linda and each of the kids hugs of thanks. I just got one of those looks a guy gives another guy when, well, you know, he wants to say more thanks than he dares.

With the gifts out of the way, everyone was ready to eat. Linda and Abby had put together a feast that impressed even Mrs. C. It took both leaves in the round oak table to hold it all. The central feature was the Christmas ham. Rounding out the offerings were potatoes, gravy, salads, and Mrs. C's yams and cranberries. And another pumpkin pie, courtesy of Abby. Under it all, was Linda's best linen tablecloth. Everyone had a place card, courtesy of the children. Mrs. C's eyes fairly popped out of her head as Linda brought out the china and silver. Linda had done it—she had *impressed* Mrs. C.

We asked Silas if he would mind saying grace, and, to our surprise, he obliged us without as much as a grumble. Georgie seemed clueless about what to do during grace, but Sammy instructed him in a whisper that we all heard around the table. Conversation during dinner was minimal due to mouths being full and eyes fixed on Georgie, who ate as if it would be his last chance; what he lacked in manners, he more than made up for in appreciation. Actually, we all ate until we were ready to burst. When we finally came up for air, it was too tempting not to ask Georgie for his reaction to the day. His answer was only a broad smile and a large burp, which even got a chuckle from Mrs. C (after she corrected him, of course).

At first I thought Linda was rolling her eyes at Mrs. C's admonishment of Georgie, but then she blanched and slumped forward. As Mrs. C yelled "Linda!" Abby caught her mother, preventing her from landing face down in her plate. Silas sprang into action, retrieved smelling salts from his pocket, and ordered Nate to run next door for his doctor's bag. Abby and I helped Linda to the parlor, where Mrs. C did her best to make her comfortable. With Linda sitting up and mainly alert, Silas assured her she had just fainted and that she would be fine, but his tone was not convincing to me. He asked her to remain on the couch and told Mrs. C to keep an eye on her. He whisked me into the kitchen and closed the door. "Joe, how far along do you think she is?" he began. I almost laughed as I explained that it was impossible that Linda could be pregnant.

Silas' brow furrowed deeply. "Has she been sick recently?"

"No. She has been tired off and on, but she seems to bounce back—mostly," I offered. "What is it, Silas? What's wrong with her?"

"Has she had to urinate more often than usual lately?" Silas continued.

"Well, yes, I guess so. But only because she's always drinking water." At that, Silas face fell.

"What is it, Silas? What's wrong?"

Silas paced across the kitchen and gazed out the window. Removing his glasses, he rubbed his face as if waking from a long nap. After what seemed like an eternity, he turned to me. "I can't be sure until I run a test, but Joe, I think Linda might have diabetes."

I think my face almost broke into a smile at the relatively good news. "So you don't think it's something more serious?"

Silas looked at me with those brown eyes shinny with tears and grabbed my arm. "Joe! There's no cure for diabetes."

"I know, but she'll just need to go on insulin won't she," I explained as I paced. "You know, shots every day. That's not a big deal for Linda, she's a nurse," I went on as if I actually believed my own words. "She can just…I mean she's a nurse…" I choked on my words.

"Joe, all I can do is put her on a starvation diet. To prolong…" Silas started, but I interrupted.

"No! What she needs is insulin! You have to help her get it. My God, Silas you're a doctor. You have contacts. You know people. You…" Again, I choked.

Silas turned me around and looked into my eyes. "There isn't any *insulin!* All she can do is limit the amount of food she takes in and try to keep her pancreas working as long as possible. I'm sorry, Joe, but I can't work miracles. I'm not God."

I slumped into a chair and tried to deny what I had heard. Finally, I asked, "What will happen to the kids if Linda, I mean without Linda they'll…" I put my head between my knees and tried to remain conscious. Finally I looked up and asked bluntly "How long, Silas? How long does she have? How long do we have to get her back to 2009?"

However, Silas had moved on. "The first thing I need to do is run that test. If it confirms diabetes, there's a specialist at the university medical school in Iowa City. If anyone would know of any other treatments, he would. You need to take her there on the train as soon as he can see her." He scribbled the name and address of the specialist on paper and handed it to me as he helped me up from his chair. "You have to be strong, Joe. Your family needs you!" He walked me to the door and paused briefly with his hand on the doorknob. Then as if being forced to repeat some horrible oath, he said quietly, "Three to six months Joe. I'm very sorry!"

CHAPTER 14

Silas did run the test, and as we feared, it confirmed that Linda's blood sugar was way outside the normal range, which Linda insisted meant she was "pre-diabetic," and did not have full-blown diabetes; but I was not at all relieved and neither was Silas. He ordered her to immediately go on a diet high in "animal food" (fats and meat) and to almost totally avoid "vegetable matter" (starches like bread and grains). Linda disagreed on medical as well as culinary grounds, but with Abby and Nate swearing to help me supervise her every bite, she quickly realized she had no choice but to follow doctor's orders.

As soon as I was up and dressed the next morning, I headed for the Western Union office at 101 East Main Street and sent a wire to the specialist in Iowa City. He agreed to see Linda on Monday afternoon. I wanted to make the trip with Linda alone, but in the end,

Mrs. Clark insisted on caring for Sammy Jo, so I purchased four tickets on the first train heading for Iowa City.

Nothing about the morning of December 27 gave us any reason to be hopeful. The sun failed to appear in person, sending instead only a gray sky filled with clouds and the promise of cold and snow. We were all thrilled to find that the passenger cars of the day had little heat at best and usually none of that. The conductor took pity on Linda when he realized she was making a trip to a specialist and provided her with a pillow and blanket. The rest of us took turns huddling under it with Linda to share our warmth.

While travel by rail in 1909 was probably the preferred method, it left a lot to be desired. True, we didn't have to submit to long waits before boarding (actually, the train barely slowed to a stop before pulling out of the station again) and no one offered to frisk us or search our belongings, but the accommodations were far from comfortable. Once we were underway, we were in for a bone-jarring, lurching ride that threatened to come to an end at any time. The train stopped to pick up passengers, mail, or even a farmer's cream or eggs at every crossing. Between Quarry and Dillon, we stopped twice for cows on the track.

Eventually we made our way through the villages of Montour, Chelsea, Belle Plaine, Luzerne, Blairstown, Watkins, Norway, and Fairfax before reaching Cedar Rapids. As we changed trains and pulled out of Cedar Rapids at 10:30, the sun came out and warmed us slightly through the car windows. Only Swisher, Cou Falls, North Liberty and Oakdale stood between us and the specialist in Iowa City. Linda perked up a bit and even pushed her blanket aside. Things were looking up.

We ate a quick lunch at the hotel across from the Iowa City train station, making certain that Linda consumed only protein and water. During the hack ride to the doctor's office, we chattered nervously about the sights of Iowa City, but made no mention of Linda's impending examination. We all hoped that he would declare Silas' diagnosis to be in error or offer some miracle cure for her, but I think we prepared ourselves for something worse.

When we entered the doctor's office, the nurse was expecting us and took Linda back to the examining room before she could remove her coat. Linda and I both insisted that I accompany her, and the nurse finally caved in when the doctor nodded his agreement. Nate and Abby sat uneasily in the waiting area.

The doctor's exam amounted to a skimpy physical by Linda's standards. She tried to tell him information about her condition and suggested additional tests that might aid in clarifying his diagnosis. But Linda, being the patient, a female, and a nurse, had three strikes against her and may as well been mute. In fact, he addressed his questions to *me* and ultimately told *me* his conclusions. Unfortunately, he agreed with Silas completely. Linda had diabetes, an advanced case.

He tweaked Silas' diet recommendations slightly, laying out an actual plan giving measured amounts of specific foods per meal and per day according to Linda's ideal weight. His prognosis used the word "prolong" but not the words "manage" or "treat." He did not have any magic treatment or anything else to give us hope.

Effectively, he handed Linda a death sentence. As we ended the session and prepared to leave his office, he summarized by saying, "She's in pretty good health generally, but her blood sugar is extremely high. I would hope that if she follows the diet strictly and stays clear of starches and sugars, she could expect to live another three to six months. Rigorous exercise every day would also be good for her. Give my regards to Dr. Fischer." As he walked away, he did apologize for not being able to help Linda more; he did *not* apologize for being an asshole.

We did not tell Abby or Nate what the doctor said and they did not ask; his prognosis was in our faces. The same gray pallor we had seen after Silas' tests had replaced the semiglow that had appeared on Linda's face on the train. I knew that Linda was feeling the weight of not one death sentence but four, and I was determined to get us back to 2009 as soon as possible.

We left the doctor's office and took a hack directly back to the train station instead of seeing the sights of Iowa's first capital city as we had planned. We maintained radio silence for the entire 15-minute ride and for the first few minutes after we took our place on the waiting area benches. When the silence was finally broken, it was Linda who first spoke, trying desperately to convince us life would, could, go on normally. "We still have leftover ham we should eat tonight. I could make some ham and bean soup if you think that sounds good. How about it, nice hot soup tonight?"

None of us knew what to say and we certainly had no appetite, but we nodded in agreement anyway. Linda went on. "Unless we get home really late, I expect you two to be responsible for all your homework reading before lights out tonight,". Her voice broke. "You're going to have to take on a lot of responsibility from now on—you know I'm not going to…" Linda choked on her words and let her emotions out for the first time, bursting into uncontrollable sobs. We wrapped our arms around her in one huge hug and tried to comfort her, united in our one thought—that Linda's time and all three of her children depended on our return to 2009 before diabetes ended her life. We drew many stares and strange looks from the other waiting passengers, but we barely took notice. For the moment, we were one big sobbing mass and nothing else but our being close and hugging mattered to us at all. I was glad that we had spared Sammy this moment, but I wanted desperately to wrap my arms around her too.

I don't remember hearing the call announcing the arrival of our train or even making the trek to the boarding platform or climbing the steps. By the time the fog lifted from my brain, we were well on our way out of Iowa City and almost to Oakdale. I tried to make my brain focus on some sort of plan I could concoct to force us back to our time, but even when I could concentrate briefly, everything I came up with was some variation on pray and wait. Questions of why and how continued to dumbfound me; I was frozen by stark fear on top of that.

By the time we boarded the train in Cedar Rapids for the last leg of the trip home, the sun was riding low in the gray sky once again. Every time we slowed down for animals on the track or stopped all together, I cursed the railroad silently for taking so long to get us home. As the train was rounding a bend just outside of Chelsea, a sudden lurch threw us out of our seats as our Pullman car screeched to a dead stop. I threw my arm out in front of Linda and prevented her from plunging full speed into the seat ahead of us. Abby was not so lucky, rebounding off the seat back, landing in the aisle on her butt. We heard screams briefly throughout the train, followed by the sounds of the conductor yelling orders to the passengers to remain calm, asking the women to remain in their seats and the men to follow him to the front of the train.

"Dad, were we in a train wreck?" Abby demanded to know.

"No," I assured her looking out the window at the train as it stretched around the curve. "All the cars seem to be OK. At worst it was just a derailment, probably something on the tracks." I continued, ad-libbing, "These trains are very safe. I don't think there's ever been a train wreck in Iowa." Just then, the conductor reached our car and ordered Nate and me and the other men to join him and the growing line following him, on the way to the engine.

The engineer had managed to stop the train just a few inches from a large, long-dead tree trunk that had fallen directly across the tracks. In the mud and the falling snow, they herded us over to the right-hand side of the train and gave us our orders. Using long poles provided by the engineer and fireman, and our bare hands, our throng of approximately 50 men and boys managed to nudge the tree trunk an inch at a time off the tracks and roll it down the grade out of the way. Without so much as a thank you, the conductor ordered us back onto the train, mud and all, as he scowled at his pocket watch and shook his head. We cleaned our hands and feet as best we could and took our seats again. Abby complained of a sore rear, but Linda seemed none the worse other than being very tired.

As the train chugged away from the fallen tree and picked up speed for what we hoped would be the last leg of our trip, Nate suddenly looked up at me and said, "You're wrong, Dad!"

"Oh? About what?"

"Trains! They're not safe; they're death traps!" he explained.

"Look, I know this was scary, but we're all OK."

"Yeah, right!" Abby interrupted.

"That's not what I mean," Nate continued. "There *was* a train wreck, near Marshalltown, out by Green Mountain."

"When was that?" I asked cautiously.

"I'm not sure: I just remember Mr. Philpotts mentioning it last year in history class. People were killed!"

Linda was now sitting up, listening. She had that bird-dog-on-point look in her eyes. "Nate, honey," she started slowly, "this could be *very* important. Now think, when was this tragedy?"

The recall of facts being an involuntary task for Nate, wasn't something he had total control over; she might as well have ordered him to lower his heart rate. His brow furrowed and he frowned. He looked down and to his left for a few seconds and then with a hopeful look he answered cautiously. "It was in the spring, around Easter."

"What year?" Linda demanded.

After a long pause, Nate admitted he didn't know and the pressure we all put on him during the final leg of the trip didn't help his memory at all. All he was certain of was that it happened near Marshalltown in the spring.

As we were coming to the outskirts of Marshalltown and the train was slowing down, we were sitting on the edge of our seats, ready to launch out the door and onto the platform, when the conductor stepped in the door to announce the stop. He was a handsome man in his mid-forties. Likely, he had a wife and kids he expected to get home to that evening, every evening. Would he be among those who would die in the wreck? I could tell that we weren't all on the same page on this—now that we had this information, what were we to do with it?

He held the door for Linda and then preceded her down the steps and made sure she, all of us, made it safely off the train. We took a horse-drawn hack all the way home, anxiously awaiting a time and place where we could discuss this latest theory. Once home, I paid the driver and Nate helped his mother out of the hack and up the snow-covered walk and steps. Abby went next door to retrieve Sammy Jo.

While Sammy clung to Linda and tried to tell about her adventures with Mrs. Clark, I gave her a hug and a kiss and then made a beeline for the attic. All the discussion about the train wreck had caused me to think about wads of newspaper that had been stuffed into cracks in the attic long ago. I had a nagging feeling that I had seen the word "TRAIN" in headline-sized type sticking out of one of the cracks. With only the light from the hallway to go by, I groped around in the dark, searching for the piece of newspaper. As my fingers found it, I tried to slip it intact from the crack in the wall that it filled, but it wasn't to be. The years and the heat of the attic had made it very brittle and I could feel it crack and tear with every tug. Eventually I gave in and retrieved a drop cord from the basement. Plugging the lamp from Abby's room into the cord, I strung it into the attic so that I could finally see. Although I had torn through the word "TRAIN," the headline and the paper appeared otherwise intact. Using my knife, I was able to extract the entire wad of newspaper, which turned out to be the front page of the Tuesday, March 22nd, 1910, *Times-Republican* newspaper with the "TRAIN WRECK" headline in huge letters.

Most of the front page was devoted to stories covering one angle or another of the wreck, some going into great detail about the carnage, even the condition of some of the bodies and predictions about which of the wounded were most likely to die before the next morning. I scanned through these looking for a name or fact, anything that would help us further understand is *this* was why we had been sent to 1909.

As I made my way down the steps, I read the list of those killed in the wreck, along with their hometowns. I think I was hoping to find some person of note or something that stood out, but none of the names were familiar and only part of the list was on the front page; the remainder was on page 6, which I did not have.

I reached the bottom of the steps and turned into the dining room, where Linda and the kids were eating their dinner. "I thought that 'Green Mountain Train Wreck' sounded familiar, Nate," I explained. "Look what

I found stuffed in the attic wall." I spread the fragile yellowed page out on the table as I continued. "This is the front page from the next day after the wreck. It took place at 8:20 A.M. on Monday, March 21, 1910; that's a little less than three months from now." I pointed to the incomplete list of casualties as I continued. "Except for the wreck itself, I don't see anything that stands out."

Nate slid the paper across the table and Abby started to grab it away from him, but thought better of it. The two of them poured over it looking for anything important. Suddenly, Nate exclaimed, "Well, you missed *this* then!" as he pointed to the last paragraph of an article at the bottom of the page. As Abby read the first few words, she gasped and cried out something indecipherable. Looking over her shoulder, I read the last few lines at the bottom of the page: *"The sole Marshalltown victim, retired physician Dr. Silas Fischer,"* but the story also continued on page 6.

CHAPTER 15

December 27, 1909-ZELEYA IN
MEXICO; U.S. NOT WORRIED–
Former Nicaraguan Head Seeks
Refuge on Warship

"Dad! We have to do something!" Abby demanded. "We can't just let this happen. This is Silas!"

"I *know* it's Silas! But we can't just jump in and alter the course of history. This train wreck is a *big* deal, the worst in Iowa history, affecting hundreds of lives," I pointed out brilliantly.

"But *Silas*, Dad. *Silas!*" Abby argued, lowering her voice to a near whisper as she realized that Sammy was picking up on our concern.

"Sammy, you've had a big day. Why don't you go on up and get ready for bed? You can take a bath in the morning," Linda directed. "I'll be up to tuck you in in a few minutes."

As soon as Sammy had cleared the top steps, I continued. "And let me remind you, young lady, all this has already happened! We're just sitting through the re-run."

I could see that neither Abby nor Linda was buying anything I had to sell. I wasn't either—I just didn't see any way we could justify preventing a train wreck, even if we could. They just sat there rereading the line at the bottom of the newspaper page.

"OK, I get that we shouldn't get involved in trying to alter history and that all this has already happened— *once*!" Nate pointed out. "But we're talking *Silas Fischer*; he's been like a grandfather to Sammy, to all of us! Haven't we already altered history just by being here?"

I knew Nate had made a good point; we all did. Then Linda moved in to close. "Joe, Nate's right, we've *already* tinkered with history by being in his life."

"Mommy, I'm ready," Sammy called from the top of the stairs. As Linda tried to stand to go tuck her in, she grabbed the chair for support and wobbled unsteadily. I caught her until she regained her balance.

"Nate, Abby, take care of the dishes and put things away. I'll help your mother upstairs," I directed.

"Who knows how much we may have already changed his life?" Linda continued. "He's over 70 years old. He has no family except Mrs. Clark. How much more harm could it cause if we keep him from dying on that train?"

"And we don't have to interfere with the train; we just have to keep him from getting on it that morning," Abby clarified.

They were *all* right. It probably *wouldn't* cause the earth to wobble off its axis if we prolonged the life of one old man for a few more years. Even one as stubborn and headstrong and lovable as Silas. All we had to do was change his mind about getting on a train. Should be a piece of cake. I paused reflectively as much to maintain my own illusion that *I* was in charge of the family as to decide the next move. "All right, so let's say we decide to interfere and keep Silas away from the train on March 21st. How are we going to do that? Just tell him, 'Silas, don't take any train trips today or you'll die?'" I taunted.

"Joe!" Linda scolded. "It's more than two months from now. We don't have to figure that out tonight! We can work on a plan in the morning."

I helped Linda up the steps and over to Sammy's bed. As I waited in the doorway and listened to Linda read one of Sammy's stories, I was envious of Sammy. It was one with a happy ending, where everything worked out the way it should. One that put Sammy's little mind at ease and helped her drift off to sleep. I wished I had such a tonic to ease my mind about Linda's health, about my family's future, Silas, everything. However, I knew if we were going to have a happy ending, it would be up to us to write it.

Sleep was hard to come by that night; I couldn't get my mind off Silas and the wreck. I rehearsed dozens of scenarios in which we tried to trick Silas into staying away from the train, but they all ended the same way—with Silas telling us we were "daft" and doing exactly what he wanted to. When I did drift off to sleep, I was jolted awake by vivid dreams about the wreck, dreams which featured bodies strewn amongst the splinters of train cars. Silas was always there, although I wouldn't allow my mind to depict him among the dead, but rather just as a detached spectator.

Linda and the kids didn't fare much better apparently, judging from the bags under their eyes the next morning. Nate and Abby had their own ideas of ways to keep Silas safe and each presented the relative merits of their ideas over breakfast as the other declared it some variation of "stupid." The whole meal reminded me of a school board meeting—plenty of heated discussion, but nothing was decided except to meet and discuss things again.

Because school wasn't due to start again for another week, everyone slept in but me. I didn't blame them. The thermometer read 5° below, but the wind knocked that down to at least 20° below. If this was any indication, we were in for a long, cold winter. I anticipated spending the day in the seat of the lumber wagon hauling boards all over Marshall County. At least I had my mittens and "hot" hat.

I rode the streetcar to 2nd Avenue and then headed south toward the lumberyard and certain frostbite. Apparently, Fred did have a heart because he didn't have me make any deliveries all morning; he *did* keep me out in the yard, restacking boards, while he did paper work in the warmth of the office. By 11:30, it had warmed up to a balmy 10° above and Fred handed me an order for delivery, but fortunately, it was only a few blocks across town. I finished loading the order just before noon and went inside the yard office to warm up.

I thawed my backside and warmed my fingers and toes on the wood stove in the office. As I reheated my soup, I noticed Fred was in a particularly good mood.

He was fiddling with several coins, almost as if he were practicing a magic trick, maybe some gimmick to impress his customers. Knowing Fred, if people ever saw him make his *own* money *disappear,* it would be a truly memorable trick.

I watched him for a few moments as he manipulated the coins; whatever he was doing, he wasn't very good at it.

"What you doing there, Fred?" I asked.

"Oh, just messing with coins. I tell you, I saw him do it with my own eyes but I have no idea how. I can't palm even two and he palmed almost 60. Damnedest thing I ever saw!"

"Who, Fred?"

"Downs! Last night at the Odeon!" Fred replied almost indignantly.

"Who?"

"T. Nelson Downs," he shot back, "The King of Coins!" Not seeing any improvement in the dumb look on my face, he went on. "He's only the most famous person Marshalltown has ever produced. Are you telling me you never heard of him?"

"Oh, him!" I pretended. "Well, sure, I've *heard* of him? I've just never seen him perform. Where'd you say you saw him?"

"At the Odeon Theatre, just up the street. He's back in town for a few days staying at the Pilgrim and agreed to give two performances; the last one's tonight. Best show you'll ever see for two bits."

"Well, thanks, we might just have to do that." I finished my soup and retrieved my mittens and hat from the bench near the stove. The dread I was feeling must have bled through to my face as Fred called me back into the office just as I was opening the door to the yard.

"Say, I just wanted you to know that as soon as we have a thaw and get rid of some of this snow, we'll have to start on that delivery to the Anderson farm West of town. I'll need you every day, long days at that, until we're done," he said, leaving the coins for a moment.

"Until we're done? How big an order is it?" I asked.

"Biggest I've had in a while, nearly 10,000 board feet. You and I both working on it will probably take most of a week," he explained.

"10,000! What's he building, a barn?" I complained.

"Yep. A big one. Probably be at it most of the spring unless he gets help from the neighbors. Not a bit too soon since they'll all be birthing about then."

My curiosity up, I had to ask, "What's he raise?"

"You name it! Cattle, sheep, hogs, goats, chickens, ducks. If it walks and poops, Anderson will be up to his neck in its babies by the first of April. Damnedest thing you ever saw."

"And I thought that was T. Nelson Downs," I challenged.

"Huh?" Fred replied, followed close by "Smart ass!" when he noticed my wink. I ducked out the door with my mittens and hat and left Fred to practice his coin tricks. As I left the office, the bright December sun made me think of spring, but a brisk wind reminded me it was still a long way off. I climbed up into the lumber wagon and coaxed Colonel and Dick out of their standing naps and back into work mode. The delivery address was on West State Street, but I directed the horses straight up 2nd Avenue for another look at the Odeon Theatre. Sure enough, the playbill indicated that Marshalltown's own, T. Nelson Downs "The King of Coins" was appearing in a "limited engagement" on the 27th and 28th of December at 8:00 p.m.

I had to admit, his picture on the poster was enough to make me want to catch his show. The "T. Nelson Downs" poster depicted a man in his early forties surrounded by an almost endless row of silver coins as well as miniatures of him performing dozens of coin tricks, all with the sleeves of his topcoat and shirt pushed up above his elbows. I assumed to prove that he had "nothing up his sleeves." Anyone who could separate Fred from two bits was bound to be worth spending an evening with.

The delivery site was only a few blocks from our house, so I swung by home to warm up and tell Linda about the magic show. As I entered the house, it was unusually quiet. Sammy was in the parlor talking with her dolls. "Where's your mother?" I asked.

"In the dining room, I guess," Sammy answered barely distracted from her dolls.

As I peeked into the dining room, I could see Linda lying on the parlor floor. I started to yell for help, but she sat up and looked at me. "Warming up any out there?" she asked as she finished that sit-up and began another one.

"What are you doing?" I demanded.

As she raised herself up for the next sit-up, she gave me that "God I can't believe you're so dumb" look and announced to herself that she had finished number 30. "I'm following doctor's orders and getting some exercise. I thought I'd go for a long walk."

"You mean that quack in Iowa City?" I challenged.

"He was a jerk, but what he prescribed makes sense."

"Are you sure you're up to it?" I asked cautiously. "It's still miserable out there. Even the horses have on long johns," I added. "And in your condition, you're bound to catch cold!"

"OK, maybe, I'll just go down to the basement and jump rope for a while, but I need to do something every day to get a cardio workout. Don't worry, I know when I'm getting tired," she assured me.

I didn't challenge her further, but just watched her as she picked herself up off the floor. Except for her color, she was the picture of health. She didn't have an ounce of fat, never had. It was so hard to believe she was even sick, let alone, well, she just looked good.

"What?" she asked suddenly, jolting me back into the conversation.

"Nothing. I was just thinking about you. And how much I love you," I answered, raising the value of my stock with her slightly. She looked at me silently in that way that said "Back at ya!" Then she gave me a big hug and a peck on the cheek. "Oh, you're cold!" she shivered. "I bet you've been miserable out there today!"

"It was tolerable. I worked out of the wind in the yard until noon and then I warmed up while I had lunch. Fred was worked up about that Downs guy coming back to do his magic act here in town. You should've seen him trying to do coin tricks. He was a hoot."

"Here in Marshalltown? Can we go? And take the kids?"

"I don't know. Think we can afford it? It'll set us back a whole $1.25." I pulled the five tickets out of my coat pocket.

Linda flashed that smile she saves for when she knows she has done something great for someone else. "It'll be good to get their minds off of everything they've had to deal with. Nate and Abby are really worried about Silas and what we can do. Have you had any ideas how we can keep him home?"

"Not really. I've been thinking about it all day, but nothing good's hit me. It's not like we can just tell him he's going to die. The shock might kill him," I reported.

"Maybe we could keep him busy with something else, you know, a ruse," she offered.

"You mean like send him to Des Moines for a loaf of bread?"

"No wise ass, something reasonable. Something he would do for someone else. For us maybe," she explained.

"Maybe a fake medical emergency somewhere," I suggested.

"Maybe. Anyway, let's talk about it again tonight. You'd better get back to work or Fred will get suspicious," Linda cautioned.

I headed out the door but turned back to offer my final instructions. "I'll be home for supper by 6. You have the kids ready and don't let them use all the hot water. I'm going to need plenty to thaw out before we go," I insisted. "And that's going to be the case for some time. He informed me that we have a big order to deliver once it thaws. He and I are supposed to be at it every day for more than a week. Oh well, sucks to be me, huh? See ya tonight."

As I headed Colonel and Dick back to the yard, I again passed by the Odeon Theatre and briefly felt guilty for not buying two more tickets for Silas and Mrs. C, but then I remembered where I had heard the name T. Nelson Downs before. According to Mrs. C, he was one of the many who had cleaned Silas' wallet after Game 6 back in October. I guessed I'd let him buy his own tickets in case he was still ticked.

I entered the yard from the back entrance and bedded the team down for the night to reduce the chance of Fred sending me out to freeze my butt again before quitting time. The yard was a sauna compared to that wagon seat. I finished restacking the pile of lumber I had been working on that morning.

When I stuck my head in to tell Fred I was going home he barely took notice, so engrossed was he in his coins. I warmed my fingers and toes one more time for the long walk home and bid Fred good night. He grumbled something about "orders in the morning" and I pretended not to hear.

By the time I got home, Linda was already dressed in her finest. She looked fabulous and insisted that she felt very much like an evening out. She had done her best to crank up the kids about the magic show. Sammy was all for it. Nate professed a "technical interest" wanting mainly to try to see how he did the tricks. Predictably, Abby saw no point in going until Linda reminded her that the theater was a great place for women to show off their finest garb. I just made a beeline for the bathroom to be at the head of the pack when the run on hot water began.

Dinner was long on protein and vegetables and short on starches and sweets, just the sort of meal to promote thoughtful conversation as the kids picked away at their food. "Dad," Nate began, "I thought about Silas a lot today."

"I did too, Nate, I did too."

"Dad, we've got to come up with a plan! We have to find a way to keep him away from that train!" Nate went on.

"Yeah, Dad!" Abby chimed in.

"I know that. I agree completely. I just don't know how to go about it. He's pretty stubborn, you know. Whatever we do, we have to make it believable enough that he won't see through it or it could backfire."

"Your father and I thought maybe we need to come up with a fake medical emergency that would take him in the opposite direction from the train," Linda explained. "Or maybe get him to do something important for one of us."

"Well, you know who that would have to be," Abby interjected as she pointed at Sammy with her eyes.

"Hey, Sammykins", I asked, changing the subject, "have you ever seen a magician before?" She just looked at me with wide eyes and shook her head, her mouth full of masticated vegetables. As always, Sammy was ready to try anything new. "Well, you need to clean your plate so we can go see Mr. Downs tonight."

With that, Sammy whisked her plate off the table and scurried to the kitchen, where she scraped the remaining vegetables into the trash and spit in her mouthful for good measure. "OK, I'm ready!" she announced.

"Sammy!" Linda barked and then to Nate and Abby, "Not one word!" as they tried unsuccessfully to muffle their explosions of approval. I took the high road and helped myself to another scoop of cooked carrots as Nate and Abby swung into action to clear the table and start the dishes before Linda could pass out penance in the form of more vegetables.

Given the bitter cold, a hack ride was the only sane option. In addition, arriving for an evening at the stately Odeon by horse-drawn vehicle had a certain appeal. We fought off the bone-chilling January cold by huddling under a very large blanket provided by the driver, the composition of which we really didn't want to know.

The Odeon Theater was actually an opera house or performing theater. I have no idea how many it held, but by the time we took our seats, it looked like a sellout. The Odeon was perfectly suited to a live performance because the acoustics were superb and there really wasn't a bad seat in the house. I was glad our seats were close to the stage however because opera glasses appeared to be the order of the evening and we had none. I saw Fred in the first row with his opera glasses, ready to hone in on Mr. Downs' technique.

A talented piano player and a drummer backed Mr. Downs' act, a duo who seemed to favor the ragtime tunes of Scott Joplin. While we waited for Mr. Downs, "The Maple Leaf Rag," "The Searchlight Rag," and "The Fig Leaf Rag" entertained us. They saved "The Entertainer" as the backdrop for Mr. Downs' introduction. When the curtain rose and the house lights went down, Mr. Downs was introduced by none other than the mayor of Marshalltown. He realized that the crowd came to see T. Nelson Downs, not to hear the mayor, and therefore kept his comments brief. He spoke only about Mr. Downs' accomplishments and fame and summed it up by declaring T. Nelson Downs to be "Marshalltown's Goodwill Ambassador to the World"! Thunderous applause and cheers of approval provided the segue for the mayor to exit the stage and take his place in the front row with the other dignitaries, three seats from Fred.

T. Nelson Downs proved to be an exceptional entertainer. From the moment he finished his first bow, he took command of the audience. Like all great magicians, he was a master at directing the attention of the audience precisely where it needed to be and away from the actual workings of the trick. Whenever I could tear my own eyes away from him to look at the kids, they had their eyes locked on T. Nelson Downs. Sammy was practically spellbound, but even Nate and Abby, the skeptics, were taking in every move he made. With each trick, their expressions revealed an increasing awe. His skill at manipulating cards and coins was masterful, but his ability to manipulate the audience was beyond comparison. It was as if with each trick, we knew something shocking was coming, but we were never prepared when it did.

Using ordinary playing cards, Downs simply stupefied the audience. First, he held a deck in his left hand and drew single cards, one at a time, throwing each high over the heads of the audience. Each time, the cards spun in a high arc and then returned to him in boomerang fashion, seeming to dive right back into the pack from which they had come. No sooner had we become accustomed to this than the single cards started dividing into two cards, one arcing to the left and the other to the right, for their return trips to his respective hands. Then he placed the deck into his pocket and immediately began drawing card after card from his mouth until he held a hand of six separate cards. Each time the crowd broke into applause (or even cheers) of appreciation, he made yet another even more impressive variation on the trick.

Mr. Downs was quite the showman, for just when we thought we had caught on to how he was accomplishing a particular trick, he shifted to a completely new category of mystification. Each time he announced a new direction in his card tricks, he took us to another level of disbelief. But the most impressive card trick of all was the "Card, Orange and Candle.'" In this trick he drew a card and tore it into eight pieces, one of which he asked a female volunteer from the audience to hold. The remaining seven he burned and inserted the ashes into an orange held by the volunteer. When he cut orange in half, the restored card was inside, missing its corner, but the piece held by the volunteer fit the torn corner perfectly. As if this wasn't impressive enough, he offered the orange juice-soaked card to the woman as a souvenir; she declined. He proceeded to dry it off by loading it into his magic gun and firing it at a lighted candle. Sure enough, the card appeared in the candle whole and dry as a bone. At the conclusion of this trick, the audience went wild, breaking into cheers and whistles.

As impressive as his card tricks were, they couldn't hold a candle (so to speak) to his manipulations of coins. Mr. Downs managed to pass coins through his knee and through the crown of a hat. He made coins vanish from sight and appear out of nowhere, but his most impressive trick of all was his Miser's Dream. In this trick, for which he was famous all over the country, he made what seemed like an endless number of coins appear in his hand one at a time as if he were simply plucking them from thin air. This too made my family beam with delight. It was wonderful to see smiles on their faces, particularly then, but it was Linda's face that seemed to shine most brightly. It was as if each time T. Nelson Downs made a coin disappear into thin air, along with it he also made Linda's concerns about her health, our children, our future disappear too, if only for an instant. When she caught me looking at her though, her genuine smile was replaced by the brave one she used to make us think everything was all right when it really was not.

At the conclusion of the show, the audience broke into a standing ovation of sustained applause. Linda and the kids were no exception, applauding until their hands were red. Just when we were sure we had convinced Mr. Downs to return for a curtain call, the mayor appeared on the stage and quieted the audience. He thanked them for coming and explained that Mr. Downs had given a particularly long version of his repertoire and had already retreated to his hotel room. This was greeted by a small amount of grumbling. However, most took it as a sign to put on their wraps and head out into the cold, Linda and the kids included. When I hesitated, Linda tugged on my sleeve. "Come on, Joe. The show's over. He's not coming back."

"I know and it was fantastic! Did *you* like it?" I asked leading up to something.

"Oh, I don't know when I've enjoyed magic so much. It was great to get out, and the kids loved it too," Linda answered.

"If you're not too tired, maybe we should go on over to the Pilgrim for a bite and see how the other half lives?" I could tell she was hesitant. "Unless you're tired. If you're getting tired, I want to get you straight home."

"I'm *tired* of being tired! I feel *good*...I was thinking about the kids."

"Well, you know, Mom, Sammy didn't really finish her supper; she probably should have a sandwich or something," Abby reasoned, always thinking of others.

"Then that settles it! The Pilgrim it is!" I ordered with an air of finality I usually reserved for my bigger decisions as a husband (like what brand of aspirin we bought).

The Pilgrim Hotel was less than two blocks away, two cold, windy, icy blocks. The winter streets and walks of Marshalltown bore no resemblance to their summer cousins. We not only fought the wind, we had to wade through snow piles up to our knees and skate across rinks of frozen muck. Nate and Abby had great fun sliding and throwing snow, but between carrying Sammy and steadying Linda, I was nearly spent by the time we reached the hotel.

The Pilgrim was the closest thing Marshalltown ever had to a five-star hotel. The side entrance took us up a set of external steps covered with a large canvas awning heaped with snow. Once inside, we were led to a charming old restaurant with walls and ceiling finished with dark panels of solid walnut. Each table had a white linen cloth. Illumination came from a large crystal chandelier in the center of the room and candles on each table. We took a corner table next to the baby grand piano.

For the late hour, the restaurant was very busy; many of the occupants had obviously just come from the Odeon and were more interested in coffee and dessert or a drink than in a meal. Over in the opposite corner several tables had been pushed together to accommodate the mayor's party from the Odeon, five men and one woman. Two of the men were tugging on stogies that filled the air with an acrid smudge (the nonsmoking section was obviously over in the next century). Doing his best not to choke on the smoke, Fred noticed me across the room. His expression said, "I know you're here, but don't come over."

Just as our waiter was taking our order, Downs entered the room and joined the mayor's group. Apparently, we had stumbled onto a private function in honor of Mr. Downs. He wasted no time in giving them what they wanted—more magic. Even before he took his seat, he pulled several coins out of the woman's hat. Then he drew peals of laughter by doing the same thing with the mayor's bald head. After a round of back slapping and more laughter, they finally allowed Downs to take his seat. During the introductions, we learned that the tall, thin man, Mr. Dawes, was from Chicago and that the woman was Martha Fisher, of Fisher Governor Company. The others consisted of Fred, of course, and three men whose names we could not make out. Mr. Dawes had come to Marshalltown to consider purchasing some of Fisher's pumps and valves for his utility business. The mayor, Mr. Downs and the other men, who were apparently from Fisher Governor, were trying to help close the deal.

While we waited for our food, Nate inspected the baby grand. He artfully reproduced simpler versions of one of the ragtime pieces he had heard at Mr. Downs' show, much to the approval of the diners. Then he launched into his current favorite Van Morrison number. Just as I was about to shut him down, the slender man from Chicago, Mr. Dawes, rose and came over to the piano. When Nate stopped playing, he begged him to continue, asking if he could sit with him and play a duet. The more the two of them played the melody, the more intrigued Mr. Dawes looked. Realizing he was keeping his hosts waiting, he eventually drew two business cards from his pocket and gave one to Nate. On the back of the other, he scratched some notes. As he left, he shook hands with Nate and thanked him. "What was all that about?" I asked.

"Beats me. He just really liked the way I was playing the song and wanted me to show him some of the chords," he answered.

Just then, Sammy, who got her patience from me and her forwardness from her mother, suddenly announced that she was going to go thank Mr. Downs for doing his magic act. Before we could do much to dissuade her, she was off to the other side of the room. Conversation stopped as she tapped him on the arm and he bent down to her level. She spoke her thank-you in tones he alone could hear, but she managed to wrap him around her finger. I started to go retrieve her, but

Linda stopped me, pointing out that everyone in the room was watching the two of them. Borrowing an egg from an eggcup on the next table, he pulled a paper bag from his pocket, and handed it to Sammy, asking her to look inside. "It's empty!" she exclaimed to the delight of everyone. Then Downs took the bag from Sammy and in plain view of everyone in the restaurant, dropped the egg into the bag. Folding the top of the bag over several times, he placed it on the floor in front of Sammy and asked her to stomp on it. Looking to us for approval, she gladly complied. To her astonishment, no messy broken egg resulted. Downs opened the bag and had Sammy inspect it. Seeing it was completely empty, Sammy whispered, "Where'd it go?" Reaching over to the next table again, Downs showed her that it was back in the eggcup. With that, he asked her to take a bow and walked her back to our table.

"You have a beautiful daughter, actually two of them, I see," taking notice of Abby. "This one is a natural at magic," he added. "Were you able to catch my show?"

"We certainly did! It was wonderful," Linda answered for all of us.

"Though I did not do it tonight," he continued, "sometimes I call a beautiful young lady such as Sammy up on the stage and have her help me turn an egg into a baby chick. Sammy would make a great assistant for that trick. Perhaps next time I'm in town. Anyway, I must be getting back to my friends. It was nice meeting you, Sammy. Thanks again." He bowed again and shook the paper bag 'til we could all hear a jingling. He upended the bag and spilled the contents onto the table, five silver quarters. "You forgot your tip money, Sammy." And with that he returned to his table.

On the way home that evening, everyone agreed that *both* magic shows were awesome and that Sammy had star potential. As soon as were home, however, we popped our little star in bed and Linda followed suit shortly thereafter. I headed for the kitchen to make hot chocolate on the sly, but Nate and Abby were way ahead of me. She wasted no time in hounding me again to do something about Silas. Again, I pointed out how careful we had to be about altering history. All the while, Nate pored over a pile of books and record albums with the business card in his hand. "Abby, we have no idea what else we'll cause to happen if we tinker with this situation," I continued.

"Dad," Nate interrupted.

"You've heard of the six degrees of separation, haven't you?" I continued, ignoring Nate.

"Dad?" he interrupted once more.

"Six degrees of what?" she asked.

"Dad! You're both gonna want to hear this!" Nate asserted loudly. He finally had our attention.

"You know that song I was playing tonight? Well it's called "It's All in the Game." I got it off of this Van Morrison album."

"Yeah, so?"

"Well, it's been covered by lots of people, Neil Sedaka, Keith Jarrett, The Four Tops, and even Barry Manilow," he explained.

"Ew!" Abby reacted.

"So what's your point Nate?" I demanded.

"Well, he *recognized* the tune!"

We looked at each other in silence for a few seconds and then I asked, "How could he *recognize* it? He couldn't possibly have ever heard it!"

"Well, he could if he was the dude who wrote it!" Nate answered. Turning an encyclopedia of rock 'n' roll around to our side of the table, he placed the business card just above a section on Tommy Edwards, the artist who I vaguely connected with "It's All in the Game", thanks to years of listening to Dic Youngs on KIOA.

"Nate, if you have a point, I wish you'd make it. It's getting late and…"

"Dad, Tommy Edwards recorded it in 1951 when it was set to words the first time. Prior to that, it had been known as "Melody in A Major" ever since it was written by Charles Gates Dawes, 30th vice president of the United States under Calvin Coolidge, the *dude I met tonight!*"

"OK, I admit this is interesting and a little creepy, but how does it relate to us?" I begged.

"It relates to us because you keep worrying we'll upset some great cosmic plan if we intervene to save Silas. I just screwed with rock 'n' roll history in a big way tonight. Charles G. Dawes didn't write "Melody in A Major" until 1911! And tonight, I showed him all the modern variations on it I know. That's what he was so excited about. Either he planned to make changes in the song or he went away thinking someone else has already stolen his tune. Either way, on December 27, 1909, more than a year before he will actually write the song, I just messed with his mind big time! And look what happened?"

Abby and I had nothing but blank stares.

"That's right. Nothing! Even though I messed with one of the most important songs in rock 'n' roll history, *nothing* happened. "It's All in the Game" came along 42 years later just like it was supposed to, and not a note was changed! Dad, doesn't this prove that we can stop Silas from dying and everything will be just fine?"

It took just a few moments for us to process it all, but in less than a heartbeat, Abby was around the table hugging her little brother for all she was worth. When she finally let him up for air, he uttered, "Geez, you two are dense!"

Ignoring him, Abby declared, "OK, now all we need is a plan. How are we going to get Silas to be out of town on March 21st?"

"I just have one question, Nate. If you're this smart, why the hell do you get such poor grades?" I demanded.

Grinning, Nate shot back, "I guess the acorn didn't fall far from the tree, Dad; Grandma showed me *your* old report cards." With that, he and Abby headed up the stairs to bed leaving me to clean up our hot chocolate mess. I didn't really mind because I had a lot to sort out. If Nate's theory was correct, we had no reason not to interfere and clutch Silas from the jaws of death. On the other hand, we really couldn't know for sure whether Nate had changed history until we returned to 2009 and checked for ourselves. The only certainty was that Silas would die on March 21, 1910, unless we prevented that. And I was sure I had a plan that would.

CHAPTER 16

January 1, 1910– NEW YEAR

RECEPTION BRILLIANT AFFAIR-

Annual White House Function to

Standard of Previous Events

New Year's Eve 1909 was no different from any other we had experienced; the clock struck 12 and the only thing that changed was the calendar. When we woke up the next morning, it was the first day of January 1910. I don't think any of us really believed that our troubles would end with 1909, but one can always hope.

As I sipped my morning coffee and read the paper, I performed my traditional New Year's Day ritual less one important part: For the first time ever, I didn't have to dread the arrival of the IRS 1040 packet. I *did* take stock of our situation. On the plus side, neither of our teenagers had been arrested, we had no mortgage, and we had made new friends. As for the year to come, all I had to do was find a cure (or at least a treatment) for diabetes, stop a train wreck, and prevent the death of a dear friend. However, that would all be in the first three months; after that, my life in 1910 should be a cakewalk!

Starting the new year, Linda was holding her own pretty well. She had lost weight, but she looked good and since she had started exercising, most of her energy had returned. The change in diet had been good for all of us, though I suspected even Sammy had a stash of snacks squirreled away somewhere.

For the next several weeks, we hashed and rehashed our plan to save Silas. Everyone knew his or her part cold, and as long as nothing unforeseen came up, I was convinced we'd pull it off. We decided early on that we had to keep our plan from Sammy for fear that the little bean spiller might leak it to Silas or, worse yet, to Mrs. C or anyone else. Therefore, our discussions and planning sessions always took place after her bedtime. Though less complicated than the plan for the D-Day invasion, by the time spring rolled around, we were confident that we had planned for every contingency. We were just as confident that this was the reason for our trip back in time in the first place.

I know denial is a powerful tool we use to survive emotionally when we are overwhelmed; during those first few months of 1910, I put a keen edge on that tool and used it deftly. I can now admit that I ignored signs of Linda's declining health. While her attitude was good, she slept longer and longer hours and was able to accomplish less and less each week. Linda's weekly check up with Silas always ended the same way—Silas smiled at her, patted her on the back, and told her she was doing fine. However, with each passing week, when he turned to look at me, he looked more and more grim. Looking back on it, I don't really think he fooled Linda either. As a nurse, she must have been aware of the steady decline the unchecked diabetes was causing. Though we never talked with them about it, we knew Nate and Abby understood what their fate would be if Linda were to die a century before giving birth to either of them. As March approached, we were all committed to the idea that saving Silas must have been the reason why we came back in time.

As night fell on the evening of March 20, except for Sammy, we all had sick feelings in the pits of our stomachs. It was as if we were on the deathwatch at some bizarre prison and all four of us played the part of the governor. We had the power (or at least the knowledge) to stop the process but through some extreme form of self-control, did nothing but watch the clock tick. We all knew at some logical level that we not only could not have any practical effect on the actual event because no one would believe us, but we were also well aware that this event, like all the others in this time trap we were living in, had already taken place. It was as if we were cast members in a very old movie the rest of the world had already seen at least once. Of course, in our case, the death hour was not 12 midnight, but rather 8:16 a.m. when the Rock Island engine would inexplicably leap from the track and set in motion the worst train wreck in Iowa history. No, we knew all too well that we could do nothing to stop the wreck, but, perhaps for the most selfish of reasons, we absolutely had to stop Silas from dying the next morning, and to do that we had to keep him away from that train at all costs.

None of us slept much that night, even Sammy. She knew nothing of our plot but remained keyed up about going on an outing with Silas. Even Christmas couldn't have had her more excited. As the sun rose at 6:04 over Marshalltown the next morning, Monday, March 21, 1910, there was no hint of disaster in the air. The temperature was already unseasonably warm at sunup. The only possible hint of what was to come was the wreck the previous evening of a freight train near Shellsburg, Iowa. The train had the misfortune of crossing an already weakened creek bridge that gave way under the freight train's weight. The engine and crew plunged into the creek, killing the brakeman and scalding the engineer, an event that escaped the attentions of Marshalltown because no mention was made of it in the paper until the next day's edition. Most accounts of the Green Mountain wreck the following day blamed excess speed, but facts, which arose much later, would reveal that many questionable decisions gave fate a hand.

Two separate trains, #12 from St. Louis and #19 from Chicago, were each rerouted because of the track closure caused by the wreck of the freight train on Sunday. Though the ill-fated engines and cars arrived in Marshalltown just before sunrise, they stood in the train yard for nearly two hours while railroad officials determined a plan. Ultimately, Rock Island officials decided to combine the two trains for the 40-some mile detour over the Great Western tracks from Marshalltown to Waterloo. They sent Mr. John White from Des Moines to pilot the two trains, a position that put him in complete control over the newly formed train.

Due to the direction from which the trains approached Marshalltown, both were oriented in the wrong direction to continue on to Waterloo once the two trains were joined into one. Conventional railroad practices never would back a coal-tended engine more than a short distance because the coal tenders (which followed behind their engines) were much lighter and prone to bouncing and derailment. They also blocked the engineer's view of the track ahead, allowing the engineer to scan only one rail at a time for debris or other signs of danger. Ordinarily, an engineer would turn the engines around to face them *forward* for a trip of that distance, but there was no turntable at Marshalltown. The alternative was to turn them around on the "Y" east of the city, a time-consuming task. White was also concerned that the engines might be too heavy for the Y, possibly damaging it and causing a derailment. To be sure, the fact that both trains were already several hours behind schedule added to the pressure of the decision.

In the end, White decided to combine the cars of the two trains in their reverse order and to run the engines backwards with the tenders in the lead of their respective engines, a decision that he and scores of others would pay for dearly very shortly. This would have been bad enough, but by running the cars in their reverse order, heavier Pullman cars were following the lighter, more fragile wooden cars. It was well known at the time that if the heavier cars followed the wooden cars and were involved in a sudden derailment, they could easily destroy the wooden cars and their occupants before anyone could take any evasive action. That was exactly what was to happen at 8:16 on Monday, March 21, 1910.

We pieced all of this together from the scrap of newspaper I found in the attic and Nate's memory of Iowa History class. We knew exactly how many would die (at least initially) from the headline and from the list of fatalities, a list that included the name of *Dr. Silas W. Fischer, M.D., Marshalltown, Iowa.*

Ironically, although we knew the risks we would take if we attempted to alter the outcome of the day's events, my family's survival required that we do whatever necessary to keep Silas' name from appearing on that list when the newspapers ran the story the next day. In essence, we had to save the life of a man who had already been dead for 100 years. Although we had read every speck of print on that newspaper scrap dozens of times and were certain we understood exactly how the disaster unfolded and the impact it had on Marshalltown, we were wrong on both counts.

Neither Linda nor I have ever been very good at waiting in general and certainly not at passing time as something this horrific or this certain unfolded. Linda and I had been out of bed and dressed since 4:30 a.m. I made coffee as usual and fixed breakfast while Linda checked one more time that Nate and Abby knew exactly *what* they were to do and *when* they were to do it. Sammy had eventually stopped singing "Sunshine" to herself and crashed around midnight, so we let her sleep in as late as possible. Once Sammy awoke, Abby was in charge of getting her dressed and ready for her big day with Silas. At 6 a.m. sharp, we heard the eerie sounds of two train whistles announcing the arrival of the ill-fated trains and the beginning of what was sure to be the most unforgettable day of our lives.

Linda and I had discussed our plan dozens of times, and she insisted from the beginning that if we were going to tinker with fate by sidetracking Silas that she had to offer her services as a nurse as soon as the call came in for help. And we knew that it would. Given her weakened condition, I was dead set against that, but Linda was not going to stand by and watch her sister nurses go into action without her. In the end, we compromised, agreeing that she would only go to the hospital and volunteer to do clerical tasks, freeing others for the "heavy lifting," and avoid going to the site of the wreck at all costs when the call for those volunteers came in. We also agreed that we would have to stay clear of the depot and all train tracks until the trains left because we knew if we even caught sight of the train and those poor people, we'd probably do something stupid.

By the time the sun peeked into our kitchen window at 7:34, we could hear Silas cranking up his Model T in the carriage house. It was already looking like it would be another record-high March day, but he let it warm up for a few minutes as he loaded his camera equipment and the picnic basket Mrs. Clark had prepared into the "T." We made him promise he would not take Sammy anywhere else but to the Anderson Farm and that he was to stay at least until noon because Sammy had her heart set on picnicking with him at the pond. I didn't let him out of my sight until they were loaded in the car and ready to leave. As insurance, we sent Abby along with them just to make sure that he didn't veer from the plan and, frankly, as lifeguard because neither Silas nor Sammy could swim. Moreover, Silas never went anywhere without his doctor's bag, so we had everything covered.

When they were ready to head out, I got a hug and a kiss from Sammy and an especially long hug from Abby, whose eyes were full of tears. "You'll be fine, Abby. Just don't let him out of your sight," I whispered to her as I ended our hug. Then, as Silas was preparing to pull away, Abby announced she had forgotten something and darted back into the house one last time.

Silas and company finally pulled away from the curb in front of our house and headed for the Anderson farm before 7:45. They were well out of sight long before we heard the first of the train whistles that announced the departure of No. 19-12 and beginning of the end for 52 souls. Linda and I checked on Mrs. Clark, who was starting her usual Monday morning routine—washing the breakfast dishes, shopping for groceries at the neighborhood market, washing at least two loads of laundry, and then ironing and folding. Our newspaper scrap omitted many useful details (such as when the first call would come in to the Great Western Depot in Marshalltown for help with the wounded), but we knew Mrs. Clark couldn't possibly hear about the wreck while she was at the market. She couldn't return home to Silas' house before 8:30, and by then we could breathe easy since our Silas would be out of harm's way. Just to make sure nothing went wrong, Nate positioned himself to "happen along" just in time to walk her to the market from the corner.

At 7:55, we heard two distinctly different train whistles blowing and we watched Mrs. Clark head out the door of Silas' house and turn west toward the market.

She turned at the sidewalk and walked all the way to the corner, but then she did something we hadn't planned for; she stopped at the corner and made a face. The kind of face that told us she was going back to the house for something she forgot. Before either of us could think what to do next, she was back at Silas' front door putting the key in the lock. Linda was on it! She headed outside and scurried over to Silas' back door and pounded on it like there was no tomorrow, but not before we both heard Silas' phone ring. No amount of pounding on the door would deter Mrs. C from answering the doctor's phone.

"Just a minute, I'm on the telephone!" Mrs. Clark shouted toward the back door.

Linda pressed her ear to the glass of the door but couldn't make out anything Mrs. Clark was saying. She kept talking calmly for another minute and than hung up the phone and answered the back door. "Yes, what is it?" she asked as she threw it open. "Oh, Linda, is something the matter?"

"No, actually I came back to ask you that. I saw you head out to the store, and then you came back so suddenly," Linda said. "And then I heard the phone. Oh, I'm sorry Mrs. Clark, but I guess I'm just a nervous mother. The girls are probably just fine."

A slight smile emerged from Mrs. Clark's normally tight lips. "Yes, I'm sure they're fine, dear. I came back for my *list*," she added as she put her shawl around her shoulders. "I'd forget my head if it wasn't attached. Anyway, the telephone call was a farmer west of town. He walked two miles to a neighbor's house to call Dr. Fischer because his wife's having trouble giving birth."

"Is that all he wanted? I mean, he didn't have any news, about the girls? Or Silas? Or anything?" Linda stammered.

"Silas isn't going to let anything happen to those girls," Mrs. Clark assured her, patting her cheek. "But I'm afraid Sammy's going to have wait for another day to have a picnic with Silas or have her picture taken with baby lambs." She to reach for her handbag.

"Why do you say that, Mrs. Clark?" Linda demanded.

"Well, by the time Silas gets the baby delivered and back to town, it'll be too late to go back out to the Anderson farm today," she explained. "Anyway, I've got to get to the market before they run out of…"

"What do you mean 'delivered and *back to town*'? What did you *do*, Mrs. Clark?" Linda interrupted.

"I did what I always do when someone calls for Dr. Fischer's assistance and he's not here. I tell them how to *find* him!" Mrs. Clark shot back losing her patience. "There are more important things, Mrs. Murphy, than baby animals. A *human* life may be at stake here!"

"Several!" Linda snipped as she shot her a look that could have put several other lives in danger and ran back to our house. "Now what are we going to do?" Linda began after she summarized just how badly our plan had turned to crap. "Silas isn't even going to get unpacked before somebody finds him and drags him off to who knows where to deliver a baby. And he'll do everything he can to get the baby and mother back to Marshalltown to the hospital."

"I don't know!" I said, "I don't know! Just let me think!" Linda was right, of course. When it came to matters of medicine, Silas was very predictable. He absolutely would bring the mother and baby back to the hospital, maybe the father too, but he couldn't haul all six of them in the Model T. And he'd never leave Sammy or Abby alone with strangers, would he? One way or the other, Silas was going to be showing up at the hospital, and as soon as he did, he'd learn about the wreck and head out to the site to help. But no matter how fast he drove his old Model T back to town, he'd never catch up to the train that had already left Marshalltown, so the worst was already past. Our best bet was to try to head him off before he learned of the tragedy and reason with him, tell him the historical facts if we had to.

"I don't know!" I said again. "Let me think!" As if it would actually help, I paced. "If the train derails at 8:16 halfway between Gladbrook and Green Mountain, it will probably be nearly 9:00 before anyone can get word back to Marshalltown and they start organizing a rescue response. Even if the farmer finds Silas in the next 15 minutes, he couldn't get to the farmhouse before 9:00 and Anderson has no phone. Lord only knows how long it will be before the baby is born and Silas can return, but by the time he does, he'll be far too late to assist in any rescue efforts. I think we're still OK," I reasoned.

"Well, I have to get to the hospital! They'll need extra hands as soon as they receive the call for help!"

Linda grabbed her coat and we headed out the door for the hospital. I gave her an "I love you" kiss and made her promise one more time to stay well out of the rescue efforts.

My watch read 8:04 as we left the house. We walked briskly toward the hospital, and I hoped that the exercise wouldn't completely exhaust Linda. By the time we arrived at the back door we had hatched Plan-o-Crap Part B. Linda would keep an eye out for Silas arriving at the front door and I would watch the back. She promised to stay clear of the melee once word of the emergency reached the hospital and work only on clerical tasks. We agreed that once we found him, we would not hold back on any of the facts if necessary to keep the old guy from going near the train wreck.

8:16 came and went marked only by a burning sensation in my throat as I choked back my breakfast. I paced outside the back door of the hospital, the one that passed for an emergency entrance, and tried not to draw attention. No one seemed to take notice except a janitor who came out to empty the trash into one of the fetid barrels across the alley. By 8:30, there was still no hint that this would be anything other than a typical March day. The sun was well up over the horizon and I could feel its warmth unimpeded by clouds. It was not the kind of day one would expect to claim 52 lives. I divided my time between checking my watch and worrying about Linda. Still no sign of Silas.

Then things started to pick up. From the moment I had taken my post, I had been slightly aware of the sound of a phone ringing now and again mixed among the sounds of the hospital. I was apparently just below the administrative office; I could hear typewriters and voices between phone rings. Then things changed. The ringing phone was answered and followed by a deafening hush of quiet. Then a loud voice made a very measured announcement muffled by the closed window. Within seconds, a controlled pandemonium was unleashed. Doctors and nurses came running out the back door carrying blankets, boxes of bandages, and other medical supplies. No one seemed to be in charge or even have a clear notion of where they were going or what they would do when they got there. What was clear was that the news of the wreck was out and Marshall-town was responding as well as it could to the worst rail disaster in Iowa history. Eventually horse-drawn wagons and automobiles arrived and loaded the doctors, nurses, and supplies.

Since the burgeoning mob of wagons, cars, and medical people was making it impossible for me to effectively spot Silas, I cut through the hospital to find Linda. She was already caught up in the developing emergency, packing bandages and medicines into wooden boxes for waiting wagons. Her ashen face told me she had not found Silas either. But worse than that, she had learned that the railroad was sending a train out to the wreck site to collect the survivors and that the primary staging area for the disaster was the train station, not the hospital. As soon as Silas learned of the disaster, he would head there. If we hadn't already missed him, I no doubt would before I could get to the station. God only knew where Abby and Sammy were.

Linda stayed at the hospital to assist in any way she could and I caught a ride to the station with Fred. By the time we arrived at the train yards, the onlookers were already gathering. Hundreds of men and boys in bib overalls and pork pie caps milled around on either side of tracks, hoping for a firsthand glimpse of a true emergency. Dozens more men in business suits hung back on the perimeter, more reserved, but just as hungry for a view of the carnage. Everywhere I looked, I could see men and boys on the rooftops of the buildings that lined the tracks coming into town from the east, all hoping to be among the first to spot the approaching train of wounded or worse. I did not see any women. And I did not see Silas!

Stern-faced police officers parted the crowd with their nightsticks and whistles so the wagons of medical personnel and supplies could back up to the platform. In addition, hearses from all the funeral parlors in town had somehow arrived, silently taking their positions on the periphery.

By 10, the gathered crowd was still eerily quiet given their numbers and the long wait. As we waited, I decided to climb to the top of Citizen's Lumber across the tracks from the depot, thinking I might spy Silas from up there, but again no sign of him. Then just as I was about to give up and climb down, one of the boys spotted the smoke of the approaching locomotive and yelled to the crowd below, "Here they come!"

Instantly, the mass of people on the ground rushed the tracks and vied for position. Everyone on top of Citizen's Lumber scrambled for the ladder at once. As I pushed my way through the rooftop mob, I suddenly saw him, bag in hand, leaning on the first wagon by the platform. I called to him, but the rumble and commotion of the crowd drowned me out. Silas' eyes were zeroed in on the approaching train, and nothing I could do was going to change that. I looked for another way down from the rooftop and spotted a telegraph pole within reach of the roof.

The train was almost to the platform and Silas was moving closer to the tracks. As the train pulled in to the platform area, the thick black smoke choked off the air and all but obliterated my view of Silas and the crowd on the other side of the tracks. I took a running jump and managed to catch one of the prongs on the telegraph pole on my way down. I half fell and half climbed the rest of the way to the ground. Looking between the train wheels, all I could see was a sea of feet. I searched for an open door on one of the cars of wounded, but all of them on my side were latched. I finally worked my way around to where I had seen Silas, only to find the space where the wagon had been filled in by the onlookers. Looking over the crowd up 2nd Avenue, I could see Silas standing bent over a blood-stained pile of white on a flatbed wagon headed toward the hospital. The driver was getting everything out of the horses they had to give and then some. As I watched them disappear around a corner, I knew that I had no chance of catching Silas and accepted that I had done everything I could for him. As the crowd filled in around me, I could not help being drawn to the scene of carnage that was unfolding. Part rescuer and part voyeur, I fought the urge to rush the train car myself and yield to the fascination.

As quickly as wagons were available, the remaining wounded were loaded onto them by police officers and other men who stepped forward from the crowd. All the way to the end of the short three-car train, men were passing injured victims through the open car doors and loading them on makeshift stretchers made from screen doors from the local lumberyards to wagons or undertaker's hearses for transport to the hospital. Some of the first wagons were already returning for a second load. The word circulating through the crowd was that many, many dead were still out at the wreck site and that the train would be returning for them as soon as the wounded were unloaded. A temporary morgue was being set up.

I turned my thoughts to Abby and Sammy and the rest of my family. Now that the wounded had arrived, there was no point trying to catch a ride to the hospital on any of the wagons. I made the best time I could on foot—running, walking, and running again. By 10:30, I was at the front door of the hospital. As I was reclaiming my breath, I heard Sammy cry, "Daddy!" and my two sobbing girls attacked, hugging me for all they were worth. "Dad, I did everything I could think of to keep Silas away, but he just wouldn't listen!" Abby explained. "I even showed him the newspaper, what would happen to him, but he didn't care, he just…"

"So he knows? Oh, it's OK Abby, it's OK. Silas is fine. I just saw him at the depot. He's taking care of the wounded. He's a doctor and they need him," I assured her. "Now that he knows, I'm sure he'll be extra careful," I assured myself.

"Daddy, we helped get a lady to the hospital so she could have her baby," Sammy explained. Abby nodded.

Down the hall, I could see a very colorless Linda sitting on a bench, making no attempt to come to me. Nate had made it to the hospital after escorting Mrs. C to the store and was with Linda now. We were all together and accounted for, all except Silas.

CHAPTER 17

**March 20, 1909- "BILL" TAFT
OF YALE AGAIN A COLLEGE BOY;
President Joins in Songs of Long Ago at
Feast Given in His Honor by the Alumni**

Linda's condition had worsened. She swore she had not exerted herself after I left her at the hospital, but if I knew Linda, that meant she hadn't tried to lift anything heavier than a piano. She was weak and her responses were getting shorter and making less sense. It was close to noon and the carnage of the wreck was becoming more evident with each wagonload of wounded. There was nothing left of the usual order of the hospital. Everyone who *could* help in any way was up to his or her neck in blood. Bandages and cotton littered the floors; beds and gurneys were everywhere we looked in the halls. The air was thick with the odors of ether and blood. With all the chaos of the wreck and the wounded coming in to the hospital, there was no way in hell a doctor was going to see her anytime soon—unless I could find

Silas. I had to find the old goat and get him to help Linda.

I searched each one of the three floors of St. Thomas Hospital and the basement. He was nowhere. None of the doctors or nurses I asked had seen him and none of them were any too happy about my asking. Finally I checked at the back door where the wagons were coming in. One of the policemen that had helped unload the wounded overheard my questions and told me Silas had come in with the first wagon of wounded and had gone back with the driver to get more but had never returned. "They were looking for a doctor to work at the morgue; you know to make sure . . . Check over there."

"Where's the morgue?"

"The only place big enough for all the bodies, that vacant furniture store on South Center Street!"

I checked on Linda one more time and explained to the kids that they had to get her home to her own bed any way they could, probably by streetcar. Mrs. Clark would help them if she wasn't assisting Silas. I would come home as soon as I found him. I kissed Linda on the forehead and hugged the kids. I could tell that Nate and Abby were at least as worried about their mother as I was. She would be in good hands, hands as responsible as any *adults'*.

By the time I reached the morgue, a large crowd had gathered in front of the entrance and spread out into the street in both directions. A policeman posted at the door to keep out curiosity seekers had no intention of letting me past, but as another wagon of corpses arrived, the crowd began pushing and shoving to get a better look. When he left his post briefly to quell the crowd, I slipped in the door.

I had tried to harden myself to what I would see at the morgue while I was en route, but I had badly underestimated the carnage. Once my eyes adjusted to the darkness, I found it to contain a mass of blood-stained white sheets, but no doctors or nurses were scurrying about attending to these souls. The blood stains were a dried brown and the victims they covered were long past help; some of the sheets obviously covered only partial bodies or body parts. Because all the deceased were covered, the odors that confronted me were worse than the sights, odors reminiscent of the one time I assisted with the butchering on my father's farm. I struggled to retain consciousness as well as my breakfast.

A priest was the only caretaker aside from the two cops who were assisting the undertakers. There was no sign of Silas. The priest introduced himself as Father Gabriel and asked if he could help me. Not wanting to take him away from his duties, I declined, saying I was just looking for Dr. Silas Fischer, but I could see he wasn't there. He put his arm on my shoulder and said almost sternly, "He's a hero, you know?"

"What do you mean?"

"He brought a farmer's wife in to the hospital this morning to have her baby and saw the crowd gathered at the depot because of the wreck. He joined the rescue effort at the depot and had the farmer drive his wife and some other children on to the hospital. He kept three women alive while they were carried to the hospital on a wagon. Then he made the driver return for more wounded." The priest paused and looked at me as if wanting permission to continue.

"Yes, that sounds just like Silas, but I have to find him! Where is he?" I insisted.

His arm still on my shoulder, he walked me toward a row of bodies. "As they were racing around the corner of 12th Street and Main Street, the horse collapsed of exhaustion and the wagon upset. Dr. Fischer was thrown onto the street…," I felt my knees lock as I resisted his efforts. We had come to a body on the end of a row—a man with a big stomach and tiny feet. Even without raising the sheet, I was sure it was Silas. "No!" I screamed. "Not, Silas! Oh, God, why? Why Silas?" Suddenly I remembered Silas' words: "Who *else* you gonna ask for help, if not *God*?" I prayed, not just for Silas but for us too.

A cold chill went through my body. I felt the hand patting me on the shoulder, comforting me. "No…Joe… don't! Look, I'm fine," he said. I turned and looked up but not at the priest. It was Silas! And, he was alive and well!

"Silas!" I bleated as I hugged the old guy for all I was worth. "I thought you were dead!" I pointed to the corpse at our feet.

"I'm afraid it'll take more than that tumble to do me in. My back may never be the same though. What are you doing here, Joe? This is no place for you, for anyone really. Reminds me of Shiloh," he said sternly.

"They told me you were here," I explained, stopping to look him over. "Linda is worse and there isn't a doctor in town that isn't busy with this wreck. I was hoping you'd be able to help her."

He winced. "I know you're worried Joe, but I can't leave here until they bring in the last body; somebody has to check these poor bastards for signs of life." Looking me in the eye, he said "Joe, you know Linda is pretty much in the Good Lord's hands from here on out. Tell Mrs. Clark I said to look in on Linda and check her vitals. If she finds anything to be alarmed about, send for me and I'll come right home. Meanwhile, make sure she's having small helpings of food every two hours and plenty of water. Otherwise, just pray for her. I'll be home as soon as I can, probably by suppertime. You need to go and you'd better use the back door so that cop doesn't see you leave."

I started to leave, but grabbed him one more time for a hug. As I did, I became aware of the stares I was getting from the morticians and the cop and realized that my affect was highly inappropriate for the situation. "Hey, where'd the priest go?"

"What priest? We haven't seen any sign of a clergyman all day; they're all too busy with the dying up at St. Thomas to tend to the departed as yet! Here comes the cop! You need to get! I'll see you tonight!" With that, he turned and headed for the front door to check out the bodies that had just arrived.

I took his advice and headed out the back door just ahead of the cop. I knew I should go straight home to tell Linda and the kids I had found Silas, but I was weak in the knees from the whole thing with the priest and Silas. I was certain I hadn't imagined talking with the padre and just as certain I had heard Silas say there hadn't been one at the morgue all morning, so one of us had to be off his rocker. I was far from certain which one of us it was. Two things were true for sure; Silas had survived the train wreck and the aftermath and was out of harm's way for the time being and I needed to get home.

It was getting more and more difficult to navigate the streets of Marshalltown. News of the wreck had already brought hordes of curiosity seekers. The rescue workers returning from the site reported that the crowd there numbered close to 4,000, and from the looks of things, we had at least that many extra people traversing the streets of our city. Reporters from Des Moines and other cities were arriving (by train, ironically) to cover the story. Professional photographers headed out to the site to capture the destruction and death on film. Marshalltown was clearly not going to be the same for some time to come.

I worked my way up Center Street, darting between wild-eyed horses and cars. Every intersection I crossed amounted to another roll of the dice. The frantic race of horse-drawn rigs between the railroad station and St. Thomas hospital had ended, but it was more than replaced by sightseers trying to find their way to the best vantage point to stare at the wreck or the rescue efforts. I finally hitched a ride with one of the out-of-town gawkers by directing him to St. Thomas Hospital by way of our house. When I walked in, Linda was reclining on the couch in the parlor under the watchful eye of Abby. "Silas is fine!" I announced. "How are you feeling?"

"I've been better, tired mainly," Linda answered weakly. Her color was still bad, but she managed a slight smile. "So we did it? We saved Silas?"

"Well, somebody did anyway. He took a tumble off a wagon of injured, but he says he's OK. He's helping at the morgue now. He should be fine. Where's Sammy?"

"Nate took her upstairs for a nap," Abby explained. "She was pretty wound up about the baby and about the few animals we got to see."

"So we saved Silas and yet we're still here?" Linda wondered aloud. Neither Abby nor I wanted to take up the discussion Linda was trying to have.

"Silas says he'll be home by suppertime but he wants Mrs. C to look in on you for now. I'll go get her." I gave Linda a kiss on the forehead and hoped that she wouldn't notice the fear on my face or the tears in my eyes, but I felt certain she saw both.

Mrs. C gave me no grief about coming over. She felt Linda's forehead, listened to her heart, and took a reading of her pulse. She also asked her the standard questions all the doctors had asked since this ordeal had started and, as always, she gave answers that meant Linda was moving closer to the end. Mrs. C advised rest and avoiding exertion with her usual stoicism, but I saw her facade crack badly as she turned to leave and patted Abby's hand. I followed her into the dining room.

"Joe, I'm worried; she's really weak. I wish Silas had come home. Her signs have worsened since yesterday. She never should have gone to St. Thomas today. I know she's a nurse, and I probably would have done the same thing, but it was not wise in her condition. I'll stay with her until Silas returns, but I want you to be ready to go get him if he isn't home by dark."

I thanked her and promised to stay close by.

"You know, you two, your whole family, well I just realized, you've been an answer to my prayers." She diverted her eyes. "For years, I've been praying that Dr. Fischer could have a family to love again—and now he does!" she said, finally looking up at me. "Gabe told me it would happen, but I didn't believe it until I got to know you and Linda and the kids. Gabe was right!" she said.

"Who's Gabe?" I asked.

"Gabriel was one of the carpenters when they were building this house. I used to make him coffee. He'd sit on the back step and talk." Taking my hand she squeezed it tightly. "He told me, 'One day, Silas *will* have a family with kids to love.' He was right." Her voice trailing off to almost a whisper, "I never saw him again after that day."

"What happened to him?" I asked.

"I don't know. I heard once that he went into the ministry, but that seems unlikely." We stood there silently for a moment, each of us processing her words from his or her own perspective.

Regaining her composure, Mrs. Clark returned to her normal, professional persona. "Joe you know Silas and I will do everything we can to prolong her life, but, well, you should be thinking about what to tell Nate and Abby. You know she doesn't have much time left. I'm so sorry, Joe, but it's probably time to think about these things." She looked me straight in the eye, reached out with both arms, and *hugged* me. That tiny bit of compassion from Mrs. C put me over the edge and I lost it, bursting into sobs. Unable to speak, I pulled away and motioned for her to return to the parlor and Linda. She did so without hesitation, saying only, "It's never easy, Joe. It's *never* easy."

I couldn't move! I just stood in the dining room, staring through the French doors, watching Linda struggling to hang on. I regretted every minute that she and I had spent refinishing those doors or the woodwork attached to them. I wanted to have back all the time we had invested in the house over the years. Time I could have spent with her. Time we should have spent playing with the kids, watching them grow, helping them, parenting them. Time that I knew was gone forever.

Linda slept until we woke her at 2:30 so she could eat and take some water. Then she went back to sleep, a sleep that closely resembled a coma. We took turns sitting with her, wanting to make sure she was comfortable even though we had no idea what she needed. I kept thinking about Mrs. C's advice, and I did rehearse over and over in my mind various forms of the talk I knew I should have with Nate and Abby, but I didn't have it with them. I couldn't! I could not make myself admit that Linda's life was actually ending. From the way they hovered around me, the way they found excuses to touch my hand or my shoulder, the way their eyes looked, it was obvious that they knew anyway. Although I refused to believe that Sammy understood what was going on, she spent the entire afternoon perched on one lap or another, not wanting to be more than an arms length from one of us. No, they were definitely on a deathwatch.

Even worse than watching the life slowly and steadily drain from Linda was the feeling of utter helplessness in not being to do a damned thing to prevent it.

Mrs. C came back twice to check on her, and each time she said Linda's vital signs were holding steady, but she shook her head almost imperceptibly as she gave me the report.

We woke her again at 4:30 for more food, which she did not want, and more water, which she craved. She said very little other than to tell each of us she loved us and then went back to sleep. I was afraid she was resigning herself to the fact that she was dying.

By 6:15, the sun was almost down and there was still no sign of Silas. I really couldn't take the waiting any longer, so I decided to go after him while the streetcars were still running. I gave instructions to the kids to help their mother up the steps to her bed and went outside to catch the next car. Just as I heard the streetcar coming from the west, I heard the putt-putt of a Model T coming up Main Street from the east. When I could tell it was Silas, I wanted to run toward him and flag him down, but I knew it would waste less time to let him come to me.

What happened next I have replayed in my mind, repeatedly, every day of my life since. Shortly after I recognized Silas in the Model T, I became aware of a man standing across Main Street to the north. At first, all I saw out of the corner of my eye was the red glow of his cigarette and I thought he was also waiting for the streetcar. But, as both vehicles drew closer, I noticed that it was the Model T he was watching. While Silas was still two blocks away, the man started walking and then almost running along a course that would intercept Silas' car. Suddenly, the man pulled something from his jacket pocket and pointed it at Silas. I think that was when Silas first noticed the man because he stopped the car. It was also when I started running toward the two of them screaming, "No! No! Don't!"

As hard as I try, I really can't remember ever processing what happened next; it was as if I carried out a well-rehearsed set of actions or reacted out of habit or instinct. Whatever the reason, I intervened too late. While I was still a block away, over the rattle of the approaching streetcar, I heard two quick pops and saw two flashes from the muzzle of the gun. Silas, who had been trying to dismount his car on the opposite side, slumped and fell to the street. Then, without even a moment's pause to evaluate his work, the man put the barrel of the gun in his mouth and blew off the back of his own head.

When I reached the car, in the dim light I could see a growing pool of crimson encircling Silas' torso. His eyes still open, he clutched my hand and tried to speak. I put my ear close to his mouth and heard him say, "Borrowed time; Borrowed time." Then he was gone.

I think I held on to him for a few moments because when I finally looked up, people from the surrounding houses were gathering. The streetcar had stopped and someone was checking the other man. I heard the streetcar pilot say it was Georgie's dad.

Then I felt a hand on my shoulder again and heard those familiar words: "He's surely in God's hands now, and you need not feel bad about his passing. He died a hero you know!" And, as I expected, when I looked up the speaker was gone.

Maybe it was because I had already lost Silas once that day, or maybe it was because my mind was on Linda and the kids. Or maybe it was the words of the priest.

I don't know why, but for some reason, I did not cry. Silas was like a father to me and the best thing that had ever happened to our family. He was a decent, loving person I would never forget, but I did not mourn him that time. I don't think I was even really surprised that he was dead. Probably, I was just numb.

When I heard the siren of a police car in the distance, I just got up and walked quietly into the growing darkness. I went straight back to the house to be with Linda and the kids. Without Silas' help, Linda was in grave danger; getting any other doctor to call on her was going to be impossible for some time. And, without Linda—I couldn't even go there.

As I passed Silas' house, I could see Mrs. C looking out the front window, wondering about the commotion. I slowed briefly until the voices from down the street confirmed that an officer was on his way to inform Mrs. C. I selfishly decided to let him handle the task alone and moved on by to enter our house.

I could hear crying coming from the bedrooms. Nate, Abby, and Sammy were sitting around our bed; Linda was in the middle, pale and shivering. Steam rose from a cup of tea on the nightstand. Linda's eyes closed. All three kids reached for me, sobbing. Through the tears, I heard Silas' name and knew they knew what had transpired. I was relieved at not having to tell Sammy. By the death grip she had on her doll, I knew she was having a very hard time coping.

We hugged and cried for what seemed like forever. Finally I pulled away and sat next to Linda on the bed holding her hand. She opened her eyes and smiled slightly. She struggled to mouth the words, "I-love-you."

I kissed her cheek and asked her to rest. I promised idly to see that she got the help she needed to recover. But, even though I said it, I didn't believe it. Silas had died in spite of all our efforts and Linda was failing quickly. I felt my own numbness worsening. Sammy climbed on my lap and I just held her, (*held on to* her actually) until she stopped crying and fell asleep. And I prayed! For Linda. For the kids. For all of us. That we could just go home.

I don't know whether I dozed off or whether I just didn't have the strength to track the passage of time, but suddenly I realized it was very dark out. Linda opened her eyes and spoke. She was very weak, but she was concerned about Mrs. C. I told her Mrs. C wasn't alone. I could see out the window and into the parlor where a man and two women were comforting Mrs. C. Eventually they bid her good-bye. And as they crossed the porch and headed down the steps to the street, the wind was whipping up. I could see the women struggling to keep their capes from blowing up and the man held his hat on his head with one hand. In the other hand was a doctor's bag. I rapped on the bedroom window and called to them, but they didn't hear me. I struggled to open it, but it wouldn't budge. Before I could get to the bedroom door, Nate was down the steps and out in front of our house summoning their help.

As they entered the front door, Abby was explaining that Silas had diagnosed Linda with diabetes in late November and that she had been rigidly adhering to the diet. Once inside the bedroom, the doctor asked one of the nurses to take the children downstairs while he and the other nurse examined Linda. "I'm Dr. Simon. Didn't I see you up at St. Thomas today?"

I explained that Linda was a nurse and had insisted on going up to help when she heard about the disaster. He gave me a very stern look and continued with the exam. He asked Linda dozens of questions aimed at pinpointing how advanced her condition was and seemed surprised by her knowledge about diabetes. Much of what they said involved medical terms I did not understand. He concluded his exam and wrote out instructions about fluids and checking vital signs. Saying he'd check in on Linda the next day, he gave her a stern warning not to exert herself in any way and asked me to show him to the door. Once we were downstairs, he stopped and made sure the children were out of earshot. "I assume you haven't given her any alcohol?" He could tell from my expression that the answer was no. "Her breath smells of alcohol, because she has ketoacidosis." I know my face told him he needed to explain further, but instead he just reached out for my arm and said, "She doesn't have much time, a matter of a day or maybe hours, I suspect," he blurted. "You'd better prepare them," nodding toward the kids, "and get her affairs in order."

With that, he and the nurses headed out the door. I followed them outside calling after the doctor "Wait! How—what do I tell Linda?"

Turning briefly toward me, one of the nurses said confidently, "She knows. She already knows." I felt a huge punch in the gut, not by a fist but by something much bigger, maybe a locomotive or a *house!* I stood in the growing darkness and turned to stare at the monster that had brought all this on. How were Linda and I to know that restoring our impressive old Victorian house would lead to this? I just wanted to scoop up my family and get them the hell out of 1910. I wanted us to get as far away from the house as we possibly could. I never wanted to see it again. I just wanted my family to be healthy and safe and back in our own time.

A cold wind was blowing overhead, twisting the tree-tops as dark clouds built in the western sky. A beam of light shone on to the lawn from Silas' office. I could see Mrs. C sitting at Silas' desk, her head in her hands. I knew I should go pay my respects, offer comfort, but that would have to wait until—well it just had to wait. I had to get back to Linda and the kids. We were running out of time. And I couldn't think of a damned thing I could do about it!

Abby had prepared more tea for Linda, chamomile, just as Dr. Simon ordered, and some meat. Linda managed to down the tea and a tiny portion of food. The lightning of the approaching storm was illuminating the sky and revealing ominous clouds. Distant rolling thunder was starting to punctuate it. We talked to Linda and tried to keep her conscious, but except for Sammy, we could see that she had very little time. She asked Nate to play his guitar for her. He tried, but his playing was always interrupted by sobs, either his or ours. When we weren't stepping out of the room to hide the mixture of grief, anger and fear that gripped us all, we perched on the edge of the bed around Linda and tried to cling to what likely would be the last of us as a family. Each time Linda's eyes closed, we thought it might be the last time. The storm was competing for our attention with alternating bolts and claps as it settled in. I stood at the window and watched as the lightning lit up the skyline, briefly outlining the Marshall County Courthouse four blocks to the east. Knowing how much Linda loved thunderstorms, this seemed like a sendoff she would have approved. The clock on the Courthouse read 11:55.

I returned to the bed to hold Linda's hand and comfort the kids. After quietly hugging her doll through all of this, Sammy suddenly asked, "Daddy, what's the matter with Mommy?"

With all the fight I had left in me, I choked back the tears in my voice long enough to lie, "Mommy just needs to sleep, honey. That's all."

Sammy, reached out with her little hand, patted her mother's shoulder and started to sing, "*You are my sunshine, my only sunshine. You make me happy when skies are gray.*"

Through our sobs, Nate, Abby, and I joined Sammy in the most appropriate of anthems. "*You'll never know, dear, how much I love you. Please don't take my sunshine away.*"

By now, only Sammy could continue singing; it was all the rest of us could do to hum the tune. Suddenly, there was a tremendous lightning strike and an almost simultaneous thunderclap that made us all jump, all except Linda. I could tell by her very shallow breathing that she had enjoyed her last storm and was nearly gone. I checked the Courthouse clock again and saw that it was straight up, midnight. Through the driving rain and the thunder, we heard a dog barking outside. As I leaned to kiss Linda one last time, another huge lightning bolt struck very near our house. Sammy clung to me in fright as the thunder rattled the windows. The dog that had been barking patiently at some distance now began whining loudly at our back door. As Abby looked out the window to investigate, she yelled, "Dad! Look," pointing to the east. The intense lightning strikes seemed to be illuminating the whole city, but Abby was pointing at our backyard. A backyard with Sherrings' fence parked next to our garage—right where it was supposed to be. And to the east, the Courthouse completely gone from view, blocked by the tops of trees, very mature 21st-century trees.

"The phone! Where's the damned phone? Call 911!"

CHAPTER 18

As I comforted Sammy Jo, I realized the crowd was thinning. The silence was broken only by the sounds of dress shoes on gravel, car doors slamming, and motors starting as people left the service a few yards away. I had no answers for Sammy Jo, Abby, or Nate about "Where?" or "Why?" Linda probably would have though. "Come on kids," I said as I steered them toward the car. "Let's go be with your mom."

I carried Sammy and held Abby's hand as we made our way to the car. As Nate held the door, Abby leaned in to fasten Sammy's seat belt, but Sammy snapped, "No! I can do it myself!" Not wanting to upset Sammy further, Abby just smiled at her, patted her head, and said, "Yeah, I bet you can," and pushed the car door shut. Immediately Sammy screamed in pain. As I turned around, I could see her little hand clamped tightly in the car door. Abby opened the door and I leaned over the seat and pulled a screaming Sammy up to the front with me. I offered to kiss her fingers, but she shook her head and cried even more. Abby slid into the front seat and took Sammy in her arms, being careful not to touch her wounded hand. I started the car and headed straight for the hospital.

By the time we pulled into the ER entrance, Sammy's two middle fingers were purple and swollen. I pleaded with the ER nurse to get her in ASAP, but I think the pathetic look on Sammy's little face carried far more weight than the pleas of a father. She took us back immediately to an examination room, where we waited for five very long minutes for the doctor. Finally, a doctor in his mid-fifties dressed in green scrubs entered the exam room and began washing his hands. "Well, what do we have here?" he began. "A very brave young lady with a big ouch?" Sammy smiled weakly through her tears, and nodded. "I'm Dr. Green. Can I have a look?" he asked, reaching for her hand. Sammy pulled back and clung even more tightly to me.

Abby stepped in and took hold of Sammy's arm saying, "Sammy, this doctor is nice just like Dr. Fischer. He wants to help your hand get better, but you have to let him look at it or he can't help you. OK?"

"Let's have you sit up here on the table where I can look at it under the light. Then we'll go take a picture to see if anything's broken," the doctor explained. Sammy slowly loosened her death grip with her other hand and let me position her on the examination table. As he cleaned the abrasions and minor cut, he tried to redirect Sammy by talking. "So how did this happen?" he asked.

"Abby, shut it in the car door," Sammy answered bluntly.

"I didn't mean to," Abby said, defending herself.

"I know," Sammy said as she acknowledged Abby's accidental apology. "It was an accident."

"We were just leaving the cemetery and I thought she had her hand out of the way," Abby explained.

"Cemetery?" Dr. Green queried, looking at our clothes. "Did you just come from a funeral?"

"We went there to visit my angel, but he was *gone!*" Sammy answered, sparing us a very difficult explanation. "There was no sign of him at all!"

"Oh, I *see!*" Dr. Green patronized as he moved Sammy to the wheelchair for the ride down the hall to X-ray.

Dr. Green returned with Sammy a few minutes later to tell us her fingers were *not* broken but only badly bruised. He prescribed ice and keeping her hand higher than her heart until the swelling went down. As he was dictating his notes into her chart, he turned to me. "So is Dr. Fischer your regular doctor?" he asked. "We don't have any physicians here in town by that name."

"He was," I explained. "a long time ago." I thanked him and turned to help Sammy down from the examination table. "Come on, Sammykins, it's time we got you home," I told her.

As I did, Sammy said to Abby, "Dr. Green *is* just as nice as Dr. Silas!"

"What did you say? Is she talking about Dr. Silas *Fischer*? And did you just call her *Sammykins*?" Dr Green asked almost incredulously.

"Yes," I answered cautiously, wanting to leave myself enough room to lie my way out if necessary.

The doctor looked as if he had just solved the riddle of the sphinx. "Just a minute. Wait right here! Don't go away!" He turned around and left the room.

I was not sure whether to run or hide; I was afraid he had gone to get the psych ward people or at least a security guard, but he returned before we had time to take any evasive action. In his hand he had a yellowed envelope, which he held as if it contained the name of the winner in the Best Actor category.

"I'm Dr. Samuel Green *the third*. My grandfather, Samuel Green, was born on March 21, 1910, the day of the train wreck out by Green Mountain, and Dr. Silas Fischer delivered him. In fact, my grandfather and my great-grandmother would have both died if it hadn't been for Silas Fischer. Dr. Fischer tried to deliver the baby there at the farm, but he had to transport my great-grandmother into town to the hospital. Once he got back to town with her, he got involved with the rescue efforts of that big train wreck and saved even more lives that day, only to die later that night."

He stopped short, as if he realized he'd strayed from his original point. "But you probably knew all that. Anyway, before he left the hospital, he gave my great-grandmother *this* for my grandfather when he was older." At that, he opened the envelope and dumped out Silas' silver dollar. "My grandfather kept it and gave it to my father who gave it to me. They both called it their 'Sammykins Dollar' and insisted it that it remain in the family because it brought good luck. He handed it to me. "I don't have children and I don't much believe in luck. I think it would be great if you took it for your 'Sammykins' when *she* gets older, as my gift."

I looked to Abby and Nate for a clue as to what to say, but they were as dumbstruck as I was. I *was* able to utter a "Thank you *very* much!" to the doctor. I passed the coin to Abby and Nate for their inspection.

"You don't believe in *luck* Dr. Green? What about *fate?*" Nate asked.

"Oh, *fate* is another thing entirely," Dr. Green answered. "I don't think our Dr. Fischer had any children; where did you work with your Dr. Silas Fischer?" he asked as we heard an ambulance wail into the ER. Before I could think of a suitable answer, he explained that he had to go meet the ambulance crew and left, saying over his shoulder, he'd like to continue the conversation another time.

"I want the Sammykins dollar!" Sammy insisted as I helped her down from the table.

"Here, you can hold it until we get to the car, but then I think you'd better let me put it away someplace safe so you can give it to *your* kids, OK?"

Sammy neither agreed nor disagreed but just scrutinized the dollar's every facet with her good hand. As we opened the doors to the ER lobby, we saw Hank waiting his turn. He held his hand up high, just like Sammy, except a blood-soaked white rag covered his. "What's up with you?" I demanded.

"Oh, I got a little too familiar with the table saw, that's all," he answered sheepishly. "I should ask you the same thing. I see you have the house up for sale. What gives? After all the work you two put into that house, you're selling it?" he asked.

"Let's just say, we got enough of living in the past," I explained.

"But now Linda won't have a 'completely restored' house," he mocked, trying to make air quotes with what was left of his two hands.

"We've all been restored just fine, Hank!" Linda answered as a nurse pushed her around the corner in a wheel chair.

"Mommy!" Sammy screamed as she ran to give Linda a hug.

"Careful," the nurse chided, intercepting Sammy. "Your mom might be sore from all the IVs!" Linda lifted her sleeve to show a bandage and the nurse lifted Sammy so she could give Linda a near choking hug instead.

"Come on, Dad. Let's get Mom home," Abby chided. "Jeff's coming to take me to the lake!"

∽

As I told you, our story is unbelievable. We made it back to 2009, but our experience gave us an entirely new appreciation for the expression "the ravages of time." Eventually, we sold the house and moved, but we didn't leave town. After all, it wasn't Marshalltown that we blamed for the experience, but rather the house and our obsession with it. And maybe Mrs. Clark. Once we were home again in 2009, we were all pretty much done with the house, even Linda. I think her brush with death helped her, both of us actually, realize that you can't fill a void with material things.

And it's not as if the entire experience was negative. First of all, few people get to experience their hometown at times 100 years apart before their 50th birthday. We also shared almost a year of life with a great man and a true friend. We saw first-hand, a few of Marshalltown's proudest moments as well as some of its darkest. I learned that the thin layer of glamour and romance in which the past is often wrapped wears away very quickly once it becomes the present. And I learned that my family, whom I thought I loved more than life itself, are even more important to me than that!

As for my thoughts about why this whole thing happened, I have my theories. While our efforts didn't *save* Silas' life, apparently we did give him fulfillment. Silas used to say that he couldn't understand why some people couldn't get close to their maker "without getting all slobbery about it". He also used to say, "No one can kill a good time quite like a reformed sinner!" I guess religion was just one of the areas where Silas and I were in close agreement, so don't expect to see me making a habit of weekly church attendance. However, you could say this experience has completely restored my faith, in *faith*!

Our lives have pretty much returned to normal. Sammy found a new baby angel to adopt, Abby spends time at the lake with Jeff, Nate returned to baseball, and Linda is once again reading the classified ads every day. It seems she took a real shine to Silas' car and now wants to find one of her own to restore; something a bit younger than Silas' Model T.

What is it they say? "Anything that doesn't kill you makes you stronger."

∽

"Time is a cruel thief to rob us of our former selves. We lose as much to life as we do to death."
Elizabeth Forsythe Hailey,

A Woman of Independent Means

"I wish that it could all be written in a book and circulated through the state, so that all could read of the magnificent things that the people of Marshalltown did for those sufferers. No city of its size ever showed a more magnificent spirit of hospitality. I am satisfied that all used every possible effort they could summon for the alleviation of those who lived as well as those who were taken away. I wish I could render a fitting tribute to the people of Marshalltown for what they did, but I cannot." - Iowa Railroad Commissioner E. L. Eaton, speaking about the quick reaction of Marshalltown's citizens and medical community after the Green Mountain Train Wreck of March 21, 1910.

CPSIA information can be obtained at www.ICGtesting.com
Printed in the USA
LVOW01s2221201213

366312LV00009B/120/P